Riley had said *for anything.*

As she watched him get out of his truck and make his way to her front door, Savannah pushed aside all thoughts of her dead husband— including the guilt. Riley looked so handsome, so alive, that she couldn't keep her heart from racing, her palms from sweating.

Savannah smoothed her hand down her sundress, a flutter of nervous anxiety rippling through her. What did he have planned for the day?

He spied her through the window, and his lips curved into a smile that shot a river of warmth through her. And in that moment she knew she was ready.

For anything.

Dear Reader,

This is a month full of greats: great authors, great miniseries…great books. Start off with award-winning Marie Ferrarella's *Racing Against Time,* the first in a new miniseries called CAVANAUGH JUSTICE. This family fights for what's right—and their reward is lasting love.

The miniseries excitement continues with the second of Carla Cassidy's CHEROKEE CORNERS trilogy. *Dead Certain* brings the hero and heroine together to solve a terrible crime, but it keeps them together with love. Candace Irvin's latest features *A Dangerous Engagement*, and it's also the first SISTERS IN ARMS title, introducing a group of military women bonded through friendship and destined to find men worthy of their hearts.

Of course, you won't want to miss our stand-alone books, either. Marilyn Tracy's *A Warrior's Vow* is built around a suspenseful search for a missing child, and it's there, in the rugged Southwest, that her hero and heroine find each other. Cindy Dees has an irresistible Special Forces officer for a hero in *Line of Fire*—and he takes aim right at the heroine's heart. Finally, welcome new author Loreth Anne White, who came to us via our eHarlequin.com Web site. *Melting the Ice* is her first book—and we're all eagerly awaiting her next.

Enjoy—and come back next month for more exciting romantic reading, only from Silhouette Intimate Moments.

Leslie J. Wainger
Executive Editor

Please address questions and book requests to:
Silhouette Reader Service
U.S.: 3010 Walden Ave., P.O. Box 1325, Buffalo, NY 14269
Canadian: P.O. Box 609, Fort Erie, Ont. L2A 5X3

Dead Certain
CARLA CASSIDY

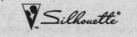

INTIMATE MOMENTS™

Published by Silhouette Books

America's Publisher of Contemporary Romance

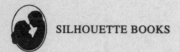 SILHOUETTE BOOKS

ISBN 0-373-27320-7

DEAD CERTAIN

Copyright © 2003 by Carla Bracale

All rights reserved. Except for use in any review, the reproduction or utilization of this work in whole or in part in any form by any electronic, mechanical or other means, now known or hereafter invented, including xerography, photocopying and recording, or in any information storage or retrieval system, is forbidden without the written permission of the editorial office, Silhouette Books, 233 Broadway, New York, NY 10279 U.S.A.

All characters in this book have no existence outside the imagination of the author and have no relation whatsoever to anyone bearing the same name or names. They are not even distantly inspired by any individual known or unknown to the author, and all incidents are pure invention.

This edition published by arrangement with Harlequin Books S.A.

® and TM are trademarks of Harlequin Books S.A., used under license. Trademarks indicated with ® are registered in the United States Patent and Trademark Office, the Canadian Trade Marks Office and in other countries.

Visit Silhouette at www.eHarlequin.com

Printed in U.S.A.

Books by Carla Cassidy

CARLA CASSIDY

is an award-winning author who has written over fifty books for Silhouette. In 1995, she won Best Silhouette Romance from *Romantic Times* for *Anything for Danny*. In 1998, she also won a Career Achievement Award for Best Innovative Series from *Romantic Times*.

Carla believes the only thing better than curling up with a good book to read is sitting down at the computer with a good story to write. She's looking forward to writing many more books and bringing hours of pleasure to readers.

Prologue

She crouched on a wooden support beam beneath the bridge that spanned the Cherokee River. Although it was after midnight, the full moon overhead splashed down a silvery light that danced on the river water below.

Shiny water, she thought. Shiny, treacherous water. For Cherokee Native Americans water was sacred, used for cleansing and purifying. It had been the presence of this river that had led her people to this area of Oklahoma many years before.

For her, the river no longer signified anything but death. Fourteen months ago, in a freak accident, her husband had lost control of his car and slammed through the wooden guard rail of the old bridge. He'd plunged to his death in the river below. At the moment his life had left his body, all will to live had left hers as well.

Every Saturday night when she got off work she came here. She climbed up the wooden support beams until she was high over the river, and stared at the water below.

Beneath the bridge the river was at its most fierce, with speed and depth and powerful whirlpools that rarely spit up a survivor.

If she released her hold on the support beam over her head and leaned forward just a little bit, she would fall. The river would accept her into its depths, and she would be rejoined with the man she loved.

Jimmy, her heart cried. If she just let go and leaned forward, she and her husband would walk hand in hand through the spirit world for eternity.

"Just let go," a voice whispered in her head. "That's all you have to do...let go." But even as the voice whispered seductively in her ear, her hand tightened its grip on the overhead support.

A sob caught in her throat as she realized she couldn't release her grip on the beam. Her heart desperately wanted to, but she simply couldn't let go. She didn't understand. All her hopes, all her dreams had drowned along with Jimmy. She had no reason to live.

Once again she stared down at the river, finding the moonlit water hypnotic. Jimmy. Jimmy. Tension ebbed away from her body as she continued to gaze at the water below. Her grip on the beam loosened as her fingers began to relax their hold. Just let go. Just let go.

At that moment her cell phone jangled from its resting place inside her pocket. Instantly her fingers tightened once again around the support.

Who would be calling her now? It wouldn't be anyone from the station; they would use her radio. Who else would be calling at this hour of the night? With her free hand she wrestled the cellular from her pocket and answered.

"Get out to Mom and Dad's place as fast as you can." The familiar male voice radiated urgency.

"What's going on?" she asked.

"Just get here."

Her brother disconnected the call, and a chill of foreboding chased down her spine. What was going on at her parents' house at this time of night?

Carefully, Homicide Detective Savannah Tall-feather climbed down the wooden beams beneath the bridge. She would not be joining her husband on this night.

She wasn't sure if she was relieved or devastated by the fact that once again she was walking away. She'd have to wait for another time to join her husband in the water she thought of as the river of no return.

➤

Chapter 1

She saw the floodlights before she got to the house. They lit up the night sky as if announcing the arrival of a carnival to the town of Cherokee Corners. Savannah stepped on her gas pedal, knowing it wasn't carnival lights that strobed the sky over her parents' ranch house. It was police lights.

What was going on? She groaned, wondering if her parents' had gotten into one of their legendary fights and some passerby or well-meaning neighbor had called out the entire police force.

Even as the thought flew through her head, she dismissed it as the house came into view. Something had definitely happened, and it wasn't just a noisy spat between her parents.

Police cars lined the driveway and floodlights hit the house from every angle. Her heart smashed into her rib cage as she saw one of her fellow officers cordoning off the porch with bright-yellow crime-scene tape.

She parked and was out of the car almost before it stopped running. She raced toward the house, vaguely aware that neighbors had begun to gather around the perimeter of the scene.

As a homicide cop she knew the scent of death, knew how the scent permeated the air at a homicide scene. She didn't smell death as she reached the edge of the yard, but before she could get any closer, she saw her brother, Clay, talking with Chief of Police Glen Cleberg.

She hurried to the two men, instantly aware that her brother was as angry as she'd ever seen him. His handsome, sculptured features were a mask of barely suppressed rage, and his black eyes glittered with a fierceness she'd never seen before.

"I'm the best crime-scene investigator you have, Chief," he said, his voice deep and filled with urgency. "You've got to let me in."

"Dammit, Clay. I told you no and I mean no."

"What's going on?" Savannah asked, looking at her brother. "What's happened?" Her heart thudded painfully as she turned her gaze to her boss.

"Dad's been taken to the hospital. He was attacked." Grim lines bracketed Clay's mouth as he spoke.

"What do you mean...attacked? Where's Mom?" Savannah tried not to panic, but something in Clay's dark eyes and in the fact that Glen didn't quite meet her gaze filled her with fear. "Where's Mom?" she repeated.

"Savannah...at the moment we aren't sure what we've got here," Glen said and stared for a long moment at the house where officers were going in and out as they performed their duties. "Apparently John Newman stopped by here about a half an hour ago. The front door was open and he knocked but nobody answered. He could hear the television on, saw that your parents' car was in the driveway and so he knocked again."

He finally looked at her and in his eyes she saw a sadness that frightened her. "When he still didn't get an answer, he decided to go inside. He found your father in his recliner. It was obvious he'd been hit over the head with something and was in bad shape. He called for help, then went in search of your mother."

Savannah's hand flew to her mouth as tears burned her eyes. "Oh, God...is she...is she dead?"

"They can't find her, Silver Star," Clay said.

The fact that he'd used her Cherokee name indicated just how upset her brother was. "What do you mean, they can't find her? She's got to be here." Savannah felt as if she'd been thrust into a puzzle and none of the pieces she'd been handed made any sense at all.

"Look, I'll let you both know what's going on when *we* know what's going on," Glen said impatiently. "In the meantime I want you both to stay out of the way and let us do what we need to do." He pointed to Savannah's car. "Sit there and I'll have somebody brief you as soon as we have any more information."

Clay let his feelings be known by cursing soundly beneath his breath as he walked beside Savannah to her car. At that moment another car squealed into the driveway. It was their sister, Breanna, and her new husband, Adam.

Savannah listened as Clay filled them in with the brief information they had learned so far. "What about Dad?" she asked when he'd told them what little he knew.

"From what Glen told me he was alive when they took him out of here by ambulance. But I'm not leaving here until they find out where Mom is." He frowned and looked at the house. "And they are absolutely destroying vital information by allowing in so many officers."

"Why don't we go to the hospital and check on Dad," Breanna suggested. "You two stay here and call us the minute you hear anything about Mom."

Savannah touched her sister's arm. "Call me on my cell and tell me how Dad is doing."

Breanna nodded, and she and Adam took off. Savannah turned back to the house, her heart still pounding an irregular rhythm. Everything felt surreal—the lights, her fellow officers, the crime-scene tape flapping in the mid-June night breeze. It all felt like a terrible dream.

What could have happened? Who could have hurt

her father? Had it been a robbery? If so, then where in God's name was their mother?

It felt odd to stand on the periphery of a crime scene as a bystander. Even more odd and frightening was the fact that the crime scene was the house where she'd grown up, where her parents lived.

"I can't just sit around here and do nothing," Clay said, interrupting her thoughts. "I'm going to check the outbuildings."

"I'll go with you," she said, needing to do something, anything constructive.

She was grateful nobody tried to stop them as they walked around the house and toward the barn at the back of the property. She had a feeling Clay wouldn't hesitate to deck anyone who tried to get in their way.

Savannah felt as if she'd jumped off the bridge and entered water so deep it clogged her brain, making rational thought impossible.

Somebody had hurt their father...and their mother was missing. Her brain worked to wrap around the situation but found it impossible to comprehend.

It didn't take long for them to check the barn, which was used mostly as a storage area for Native American artifacts. Rita Birdsong James worked at the Cherokee Cultural Center at the edge of town and had slowly taken over the barn as a place to keep items for the center.

It was when they were searching the shed that Savannah's cell phone rang and she answered to hear Breanna at the other end of the line.

"It's not good, Savannah," she said, her voice

choked with emotion. ''Dad received several severe blows to the back of his head. The doctor isn't sure about the possibility of brain damage, and Dad is in a coma. What's up there? Have they found Mom?''

''No...nothing. They aren't telling us anything, Bree.'' For the first time the full awareness of the gravity of the situation hit Savannah.

Their father was in a coma and their mother was missing. She sank down on a bale of hay, tears suddenly blurring her vision. ''Bree, I'm coming to the hospital. There's nothing I can do here. Glen won't let us anywhere near the house. Maybe Dad will wake up and be able to tell us what happened.''

''I'll stay here,'' Clay said a moment later after she'd hung up with Breanna and brother and sister were walking back toward the house.

''Come with me to the hospital, Clay. Right now Dad needs us there.'' She somehow felt it was important that they all be together, in the same place. She felt as if her family was slipping through her fingers and what she needed was to hang on tightly to them all.

Clay raked a hand through his thick dark hair, uncertainty twisting his handsome features. He stared at the house, tension radiating from him, the same tension that whipped through her. ''What in the hell happened here tonight?''

''I don't know, Clay.'' She placed a hand on his muscular forearm. ''But it's obvious we're out of the loop here at the moment. Come with me to the hospital. Right now we don't know where Mom is, but we know that Dad needs us.'' She was half-afraid that if he remained here he would do something to get himself thrown off the police force.

''All right,'' he replied. ''I'll just check in with the chief and I'll meet you there.''

As Savannah headed for her car, she noticed the crowd of neighbors and the curious had grown despite the fact that it was the middle of the night.

She recognized the Marshalls, her parents' nearest neighbors. Their house was some distance away, but they both stood by their car, worried expressions on their lined faces. Familiar faces everywhere, and they all seemed to be watching her as she made her way to her car.

She stopped to talk to nobody, having nothing to say, no way to assure anyone of anything. She got into her car and started the engine and that's when she noticed him…a stranger on the edge of the crowd.

He stood taller than most of the rest of the people, and his gaze was fixed on the house. With a cop's training, she took in his appearance before backing out of the driveway.

He was good-looking, with dark-brown hair and facial features that radiated intensity. People stood in front of him, making it impossible for her to see his build. A traveler who'd seen the lights and action, she thought as she pulled away from the ranch.

Or a perpetrator watching the aftermath of his actions, her seasoned cop brain thought. She knew it was not unusual for the criminal to watch the unfolding drama, to even become involved in the investigation of the crime they committed.

Surely one of the officers would take names and question the people who had arrived to see what was going on. It was standard procedure.

Besides, she couldn't think about the investigation. Despite the fact that her years as a homicide detective had seasoned her to maintain a certain amount of emotional distance, her training and experience seemed to have left her the moment she'd pulled up to the house.

As she sped toward the hospital, she desperately sought that emotional distance, but her hands trembled and her chest felt heavy and a sickness she'd never felt before permeated every pore of her body.

Where was her mother? Was her father going to be all right? What on earth had happened? She stepped on the gas pedal, fear consuming her from the inside out.

Riley Frazier stood staring at the house where the bright-yellow tape contrasted with the beige house paint and hunter-green shutters and trim. The sight brought back painful memories of another crime at another house years before. As he stared at the house, snatches of conversation drifted toward him.

"…can't find Rita."

"…heard his head was bashed in."

"…you know they fight a lot…"

He listened with interest as the people around him speculated on what had happened to Rita and Thomas

James. He wouldn't draw any conclusions until he heard the official word on what had happened at the sprawling, attractive ranch house.

It was possible he was here on yet another wild-goose chase. Certainly over the past two years he'd been on many. But when he'd heard the initial report of what was going on from a reporter friend in Cherokee Corners, he'd left his home in Sycamore Ridge and driven like a bat out of hell to get here.

It was possible what he was watching was the investigation of a domestic dispute gone bad, or a botched robbery attempt. It was possible it had nothing to do with what had happened to his parents two years ago.

The overbright floodlights, the swirling cherry police lights and the yellow crime-scene tape brought back nightmarish memories. The sight of his father's dead body sprawled in the middle of the living room floor still haunted him…along with all the questions the crime had produced.

That's why he was here, looking for answers to a crime nobody cared about anymore but him. This might be a wild-goose chase, but in the past two years his life had become a series of wild-goose chases.

His information had told him that there were three James siblings, and he suspected he'd driven up in time to see the three huddled together with the chief of police. The man and two women he'd seen had looked like siblings.

All had been of Native American heritage, with rich black hair and finely sculptured features. His source had even given him their names—Clay, Breanna and Savannah—and told him that each of them worked in some aspect of law enforcement.

He'd watched as one of the women and a man had left together. Then had watched as the second woman left. Finally the man he thought was Clay James got into a car and took off as well.

Riley suspected they were probably headed to the hospital where their father had been taken. He waited around until the police began to attempt to disperse the crowd and he saw the police chief leave, then he got into his car and headed into the small city of Cherokee Corners.

The quickest way to find out what had happened at the James ranch was to speak to one of the children. It was too late for any of the details to get into the morning paper, and the police wouldn't be talking to anyone until they spoke to the family members.

He had a feeling if he wanted information, the hospital would be the place to get it. He didn't want speculation and rumor. He wanted facts, and he had a feeling the only way to get facts sooner rather than later was to go introduce himself to the James siblings.

The nightmare continued. Savannah sat in the hospital waiting room wondering when they would have some answers, when any of this would make sense.

Clay paced the floor, looking as if he would gladly take off the head of anyone who got in his way.

Breanna sat next to Adam, their hands clasped together.

Savannah had been there for almost two hours, and the doctor had yet to come out and speak to them. There had been no word on their mother's whereabouts and nothing concrete from the investigation itself.

Savannah wished she had somebody's hand to hold or that she could generate the kind of anger that seemed to be sustaining Clay. Instead she was left with a disquieting numbness.

They weren't alone in the waiting room. Saturday nights always brought an influx of people to the emergency room in the only hospital in town.

As Dr. Miles Watkins, their family physician, came into the room they converged on him like a single unit. He held up his hands to still their barrage of questions. "I don't have a lot to tell you," he said when they all fell quiet.

"Your father has suffered massive trauma to the back of his head. We can't be sure of the extent of any brain damage at the moment. Our main concern has been to stabilize him. At the moment his vital signs are fair, but he's currently in a coma. I've called in a neurologist from Tulsa. He'll be here sometime tomorrow. In the meantime my recommendation to all of you is to go home. There's nothing you can do here." He sighed wearily, then added. "Go home and pray."

He'd barely exited the waiting room when the exterior door whooshed open and Glen Cleberg entered.

Lines of stress surrounded his mouth, and his hair stood on end, as if it had felt a frustrated hand rake through it more than once. He motioned them to chairs in a corner and joined them there.

"I know you're all anxious to learn what we've uncovered so far." He frowned, as if dreading what information he had to impart. Every nerve ending in Savannah's body screamed with tension.

"It looks like a domestic dispute scene that got out of control," the chief told them.

"That's crazy," Clay said, voicing Savannah's initial response.

"Chief, surely you don't think our mother could be responsible for Dad's condition?" Savannah looked at him incredulously.

His frown deepened. "I'm just telling you what the initial investigation points to. There's no sign of forced entry, no indication that anything has been stolen."

"How would you know if anything has been stolen?" Breanna asked, tears shimmering in her eyes.

"Tomorrow, after the crime-scene investigators get finished, we'll do a walk-through," Glen said. "I need you all to tell me if you see something out of place. But, I can tell you right now the only things that appear to be missing are a suitcase from a set in your parents' closet and some of your mother's personal items."

Stunned. His words stunned them all. Savannah could see the shock she felt on her siblings' faces. The implication was obvious. They believed that Rita had smashed her husband over the head, then packed her bags and run.

"Glen, you know my parents, you know what you're thinking is impossible," she said.

He hesitated a moment. "I know what the evidence looks like at the moment," he replied softly.

"Then let me inside. Let me find the evidence that points to the truth," Clay exclaimed, his hands balled into fists at his sides.

"That's exactly what I'm not going to let happen," Glen said, his tone sharp. "Even though the three of you are officers of the law, you will have nothing to do with this investigation." He held up a hand to still the protests that came at him from three different directions.

"Think about it. I can't let the family members of a crime do the investigating of the case. A defense attorney would be able to rip a case to shreds under those circumstances."

Savannah knew he was right, but that didn't make the situation any easier to swallow. "But what about Mother's car?" she asked suddenly. "It was there in the driveway...so how did she leave?"

"I don't have the answers," he said with obvious frustration. "Look, we're only a couple of hours into this investigation. We have a lot of work ahead of us. It would help if your father could enlighten us about what happened."

"Dad's in a coma," Clay said, and his voice radiated with the hollowness of a person still in shock.

''According to Doc Watkins he isn't going to be explaining anything anytime soon.''

For the first time since she'd driven up to her parents' house a stark grief swept over Savannah. She felt almost sick to her stomach as she tried to digest what they knew so far.

The man who had held her when she'd been sick, the man who had taught her how to dance, how to shoot a gun and given her a love for law enforcement was clinging to life by a thread.

Her mother, a proud, beautiful woman who had taught her to honor her Cherokee heritage, the woman whose hands had soothed, whose laughter could light up the night, was missing.

Hold on, Daddy, she cried in her heart. Please hold on, we still need you. Where are you, Mom? What has happened to you?

''Savannah, why don't you meet me at your folks' place tomorrow at noon. We'll do a walk-through then,'' Glen said. ''I'm putting an all points bulletin out on your mother. We need to find her. We need to talk to her. Take the next couple of days off. Your father is going to need you when he comes out of his coma, and I don't want any of you mucking around in this investigation.''

''If he thinks I'm staying out of this, he's crazy,'' Clay said the minute Glen had left to go in search of Dr. Watkins.

''Just because we can't investigate officially doesn't mean we can't investigate unofficially,'' Breanna said.

"I can't stand around here and do nothing," Clay replied. "I'm going to make some phone calls, drive around and see if I can find Mom. Maybe she got hit in the head, too...has wandered off in a daze and doesn't know who or where she is."

"You know she didn't have anything to do with Dad's injuries," Savannah said.

"That goes without saying," her brother replied. He looked toward the windows. "She's out there somewhere, and she's in trouble. We've got to find her."

He didn't wait for any reply but strode out the door and disappeared into the night.

Savannah felt the darkness of the night closing in around her, filling her heart, filling her soul with fear. She turned back to look at her sister. Breanna reached out and grabbed her into a hug that kept the darkness from consuming her.

"Go," Breanna said as she released her. "Go find Mom. Adam and I will stay here."

"You'll call me if there's any change?" she asked.

"Of course we will," Adam said as he wrapped an arm around his wife's shoulder.

Although she was reluctant to leave, Savannah knew there was nothing she could do here. Her father was getting the care he needed.

She left the hospital through the emergency room doors and stopped in her tracks. Parked in a car in the closest parking space to the door was the handsome stranger she'd seen out at her parents' place.

Who was he? What was he doing here? It had been

odd enough to see his strange face among those of the neighbors at the house. Had he been involved in whatever had happened there? Had he come here in a compulsive, sick need to see the grief he'd caused? Was he here to see if her father had come awake and was talking?

A burst of adrenaline chased away grief as she pulled her handgun from her shoulder holster and approached the car. "Show me your hands," she demanded to the man in the driver seat.

Startled blue eyes widened as he lifted his hands off the steering wheel. "I think there's been some sort of mistake." His voice was a deep baritone.

"The only mistake anyone has made around here is yours." She pulled open the driver door. "Now, get out of the car, put your hands on the roof and spread 'em."

Chapter 2

Riley Frazier hadn't reached the age of thirty-four without learning when to balk and when to comply. When a woman who'd just suffered an emotional trauma pointed a gun and began to bark orders, it was definitely a good idea to comply.

He got out of his car, placed his hands on the roof and spread his legs. "There's a wallet in my back pocket with my identification in it," he offered.

She frisked him with a professional, light touch, beginning at his ankles. She patted up his legs, then around his waist. Only then did she pluck his wallet from his back pocket.

He remained in place, although there were a million things he wanted to say to her, things he wanted to ask her.

"What are you doing here, Mr. Frazier?" she asked.

He dropped his arms to his sides and turned to face her. In the bright illumination of the parking lot light overhead he got his first good look at her. A rivulet of pleasure swept through him.

Earlier at her parents' house he'd been too far away to see just how beautiful she was. Long black lashes framed dark eyes. Her hair was jet-black, and the short cut emphasized high cheekbones and sensual lips.

She stared at him expectantly and he frowned, unable to remember her question to him. "I'm sorry... What do you want to know?"

"Your identification says you're from Sycamore Ridge. What are you doing here in Cherokee Corners and what were you doing out at my parents' ranch?"

Riley suddenly realized what it looked like...why his presence had prompted her to pull a gun and check him out. "It's not what you think."

"And how do you know what I think?" she returned in a cool tone as she handed him back his wallet.

"I know what I'd be thinking if I was in your place," he replied.

"Riley!"

They both turned at the sound of the young male voice. Scott Moberly hurried toward them, and Riley thought he heard a faint groan come from Savannah.

Scott reached them, half-breathless from his run across the parking lot. "You bothering the local law enforcement, Riley?'' Scott asked, a wide grin stretching across his freckled face.

Riley shrugged, and Scott turned his attention to the woman officer as he withdrew a notepad and pen from his pocket. ''So, what's the scoop, Savannah? Is your father dead?''

''Scott!'' Riley exclaimed as Savannah's features twisted with a combination of pain and anger.

''Oh…was that insensitive? Sorry.'' Scott sighed miserably. ''How about an exclusive, Savannah?''

''I'll give you an exclusive. All reporters are pond scum.'' She turned on her heels and started toward her car.

She'd written him off as a reporter, Riley thought. He fumbled in his wallet and withdrew his business card and a copy of a newspaper clipping.

''Savannah,'' he shouted, and ran after her. She didn't stop walking, didn't indicate in any way that she had heard him.

He caught up with her at her car. ''Savannah…wait.''

She whirled around to face him, her eyes flashing dark fires of anger. ''No interview, no scoop…I have nothing to say.''

''Please…*I'm* not a reporter,'' he said quickly. She jumped in surprise as he grabbed her hand and pressed his card and the copy of the clipping into her palm. ''Call me when you're ready to talk.''

He backed away and watched as she got into her car and drove out of the hospital parking lot. He hoped she'd call. He hoped she'd read the old news clipping, but there were no guarantees. For all he knew she might toss what he'd given her into the trash without even looking at it.

"Did she say anything to you?" Scott asked eagerly as Riley returned to where he stood.

"No, nothing." He turned and looked at the young man he'd befriended two years earlier. "Thanks for calling me."

Scott nodded. "As soon as I heard the initial report, I knew you'd want to know." Scott glanced longingly at the emergency room door.

"Go on, Scott," Riley said. "Go see if you can get a story, but try to be a bit more sensitive. Anyone you find to talk to about any of this will be in shock…in pain."

Scott flashed him another quick grin. "Got it." As he disappeared into the hospital, Riley sat on a nearby bench, not yet ready to make the hour-long drive back to his home in Sycamore Ridge.

The late-June night air was unusually warm, more in keeping with August than June. It had been on a hot August night that his world had been ripped asunder, and for the past two years he'd felt as if his life had been in limbo.

He'd awakened each morning with unanswered questions plaguing his mind and had gone to bed each night with those same questions still begging for answers.

He'd met Scott in the dark days following the event that had shattered his life. The brash young reporter had journalistic dreams of becoming the next Ann

Rule and writing bestselling books about compelling crimes.

Initially Riley had found the young man relentless and his questions an irritating breach of good manners and an invasion of Riley's privacy.

But when the cops had gone away, when the crime-scene investigators had packed up and gone home, Scott had remained. When the neighbors had stopped sending cards of condolence and the flowers on his father's grave had withered and blown away, Scott was still around, sometimes asking insensitive questions but also offering friendship and support that Riley desperately needed at the time.

The friendship had lasted, although there were times when Scott's eagerness overwhelmed his tact. And tonight with Savannah had been one of those times.

He turned his head as he heard the hospital door open and Scott walked through. He spied Riley and walked over and sat next to him on the bench.

"What did you find out?" Riley asked.

"Not much," Scott replied glumly. "Thomas James is still alive, but he's in a coma. I tried to get some information out of Glen Cleberg, the police chief, but he wouldn't tell me anything. It's going to be hell trying to get any information from law enforcement...you know, the brotherhood of cops, the blue wall and all that."

"I think that's only a myth when a cop is supposed to be bad or corrupt," Riley replied.

"Who knows what was going on with Thomas.

You know he was chief of police before Glen Cleberg. Maybe somebody had a score to settle with him.''

"And so they banged him over the head and did what with his wife?'' Riley asked.

"I don't know,'' Scott admitted. "I'm just speculating here.''

"I thought good reporters weren't allowed to speculate. I thought they were just supposed to report the facts.''

Scott grinned widely, exposing a chipped front tooth. "Who ever told you I was a good reporter?''

"So, tell me about Savannah James,'' Riley asked, changing the subject.

"Her name is actually Savannah Tallfeather. She's a homicide dick and a widow. About a year ago her husband, Jimmy, crashed into the old bridge over the Cherokee River. The wood was old and rotten and his car went over the edge.''

Riley frowned. There should be a law—only one tragedy in a single lifetime. The fact that she was so young and already had suffered two seemed vastly unfair.

"It's eerily similar to what happened to your parents, isn't it?'' Scott asked. He wasn't talking about Jimmy Tallfeather's untimely death. He was talking about whatever had happened at the James ranch.

"Yes…at least from the snippets of information I've heard so far.'' Riley sighed and looked upward toward the night sky where the stars were obscured by the bright parking lot lighting. "But I hope it's not the same."

He looked back at Scott, but his thoughts were filled with a vision of the lovely Savannah. He knew every agonizing emotion she was experiencing. He knew intimately the sensation of shock, the taste of uncertainty and the scent of your own fear.

He knew the furtive glances of people willing to believe the worst. He knew the isolation of friends drifting away, uncomfortable and somehow afraid. He wouldn't wish what he'd been through in the past two years on anyone, especially a young woman who'd already been touched by tragedy.

"I hope they find Rita James alive and well. I hope she left for a planned trip hours before her husband was attacked." Riley held his friend's gaze intently. "I hope this is nothing like what happened to my parents. But if it is like what happened to my family, then God help them all."

It was near dawn when sheer exhaustion drove Savannah to bed. She'd been up for over twenty-four hours, and although her head wanted to keep searching for her mother, her body rebelled, forcing her to rest.

The night had been a fruitless search. She and Clay had contacted half the townspeople to see if they knew anything about Rita's whereabouts.

They had contacted friends, relatives and acquaintances, all to no avail. Savannah had taken a photo of her mother to the bus station while Clay had checked all the rental car companies.

Nothing. It was as if Rita had packed her suitcase, then disappeared off the face of the earth.

Before crawling into bed for a couple hours of sleep, Savannah sat in her living room window and watched the sun peek up over the horizon as if shyly testing its welcome.

Tears burned her eyes. Was her mother seeing the sunrise? Had she left on an unexpected trip and had no idea what had happened at the ranch? Or had whomever hurt Thomas also done something awful to Rita?

Savannah had shed few tears all night, but as she watched the beauty of the sunrise, sobs choked in her throat, racked her body and ripped through her heart.

She'd believed all her tears had been depleted on the day she'd buried her Jimmy, but she'd been wrong. A river of tears escaped from her until she fell into an exhausted sleep.

Her alarm awakened her at nine. Gritty-eyed and half-asleep, she stumbled into the bathroom for a quick shower.

As the steamy hot water washed away the last of her grogginess, she mentally steeled herself for what lay ahead of her—the walk-through at the ranch house to see if anything was missing or out of place.

Savannah had been to many crime scenes in the six years she'd been a cop, but she'd never been to a crime scene where her own family members were the victims. And there was no doubt in her mind that her mother was a victim as much as her father was. They just hadn't figured out yet what her mother was a victim of.

Before leaving her apartment she called Breanna to check in on their father. There had been no change in his condition, and Breanna told her she and Adam were heading home for some much-needed sleep. Clay had no news, either.

In the brilliant sunshine of day the crime-scene tape surrounding the house looked even more horrifying than it had the night before.

Savannah got out of her car and was greeted by Officer Kyle O'Brien, a young man who'd apparently drawn the duty of guarding the house until it was released by the police department.

"The chief is on his way. I'm sorry I can't let you inside until he gets here." He looked at her apologetically.

"It's all right, Kyle." She forced a smile. "I'll just wait for him in my car." She slid back in behind her steering wheel, ignoring the look on Kyle's face that indicated he wouldn't have minded a little conversation.

She didn't feel like talking. She leaned her head against her headrest and closed her eyes as the events of the night before replayed in her mind.

He'd had the bluest eyes she'd ever seen. Her mind filled with an image of the man she'd frisked in the hospital parking lot. Yes, he'd had the bluest eyes she'd ever seen, but they hadn't sparkled; rather, they had been somber and filled with sympathy.

She rummaged in her purse and pulled out the business card he'd handed her the night before. Riley Frazier, Master Builder of Frazier Homes.

She'd heard of Frazier Homes. But why would a homebuilder think she'd want to speak with him? She wasn't in the market for a new home, and last night had definitely not been the time to approach her. It didn't make any sense.

At that moment Glen Cleberg arrived on the scene. Savannah shoved the business card back into her purse, then got out of the car to greet her boss.

"How you doing, Savannah?" he asked with uncharacteristic kindness.

When Glen had become chief a year ago, he'd seemed to be afraid that the James siblings wouldn't honor his authority after serving under their father. He'd been harder on them than on any of the other officers and it had taken several months before they had all adjusted.

"I'm fine…eager to get this over with."

He frowned. "Maybe I should have had Clay do it…but I was afraid he'd look at the scene professionally rather than as a family member."

"He probably would have," Savannah admitted. Clay was consumed by his work as a crime-scene investigator. She suspected if somebody cut him he wouldn't bleed blood, but would bleed some kind of chemical solution used in his lab to look for clues.

"We tried not to make a mess, but you know some things can't be helped," Glen said as he handed her a pair of latex gloves.

"You don't have to explain that to me." She pulled on the gloves, surprised by the dread that she felt concerning entering the home where she'd been raised by loving parents.

Glen drew a deep breath. "Let's get on with it, then." He unlocked the front door and together they stepped into the large living room.

Savannah drew in a breath as she saw the blood. It stained her father's chair, dotted the ceiling overhead and had dried on the television screen in front of the chair. She knew enough about blood-spatter evidence to realize her father had received a tremendous blow.

She struggled to find the emotional detachment to get her through this, trying to think of it as an unidentified victim's blood instead of her father's.

Fingerprint dust was everywhere and swatches of carpeting had been cut and removed. Her father's chair faced away from the front door. It would have been easy for anyone to ease into the house and hit him over the head.

"Let me guess, no sign of forced entry," she said. "My parents kept their door open and unlocked until they went to bed." Emotion threatened to choke her. She swallowed hard against it. "It would never have entered their minds to be afraid here, to think they should lock up the doors and windows."

She drew a deep breath and looked around the room carefully. "Nothing seems to be missing in here. If it was a robbery attempt, you'd think they would have taken the stereo or computer equipment."

Glen didn't quite meet her gaze, and with a stunning jolt she realized he believed her mother had done this. He wasn't seriously entertaining the thought that it had been a botched robbery or anything else.

"Glen, I know my parents fought. Everyone knew they fought. They fought loud and often in public. They were both stubborn and passionate, but they were madly in love. You know my mother isn't capable of something like this."

His gaze still didn't meet hers. "Savannah, we can only go where the evidence takes us, and until we find your mother, she's our top suspect in this case."

Knowing he thought it and hearing him say it aloud were two different things. She swallowed the vehement protest rising to her lips, aware that whatever she said would make no difference.

From the living room they entered the kitchen, which was neat and clean and showed no evidence that anything or anyone unusual had been in the room. The only thing out of place was a pie that sat on the countertop, along with a knife and a plate. Her father loved his pies, and Rita baked them often for her husband.

The next two bedrooms yielded nothing unusual. Nothing appeared to have been touched or disturbed in any way.

As they entered her parents' bedroom, a small gasp escaped her lips. Here it was obvious something had happened. The closet door stood agape, and it was evident clothes were missing. The dresser drawers were open, clothing spilling out onto the floor as if somebody had rummaged through them quickly.

She walked to the closet and looked on the floor, where three suitcases in successive sizes had always stood side by side. Now there were only two. The middle size was missing.

She stared at the spot where the suitcase had stood, trying to make sense of its absence, but it made no sense. In all their years of marriage her parents had never taken trips separately.

It would have been extremely out of character for Rita to pack a bag and go anywhere without her husband. Just as it would be extremely out of character for her to harm the man she loved.

Clothes were missing...several sundresses, slacks and summer blouses. Empty hangers hung on the rod and littered the floor, as if items had been forcefully pulled off them. A check of the dresser drawers showed missing lingerie, sleepwear and other personal items.

She became aware of the ticking of the schoolhouse clock that hung on the wall, stared at the beautiful dark-blue floral bedspread that covered the bed.

What had happened here? She looked at Glen, whose face was absolutely devoid of expression. "I don't care how it looks. I'll never believe my mother had anything to do with my father's injuries."

"But you have to admit, it looks bad."

Savannah's heart ached as she acknowledged his words with a curt nod. Yes, it looked bad. It looked very bad. If her father didn't survive, then her mother would be wanted for murder. Either possibility was devastating.

They finished the walk-through and left the house. She'd hoped to find some sign of an intruder, some clue that somebody else was responsible for her father's condition. But she'd seen nothing to help prove her mother's innocence. And where was her mother?

She remained in her car long after Glen had pulled away, trying to piece together possible scenarios that might explain the absence of her mother's personal items, the missing suitcase. But nothing plausible fit.

So, what happened now? Where did they go from here? She dug into her purse to find her car keys and suddenly remembered that Riley Frazier hadn't just handed her a business card the night before. He'd handed her something else, as well.

Digging in her purse, she finally found the sheet of paper that had been thrust into her palm by the handsome stranger. She opened it.

It was a photocopy of an old newspaper article that had appeared in the *Sycamore Ridge News* on August 14, two years ago.

Man Murdered…Wife Missing, the headline read. Savannah's heartbeat raced as she read the article that detailed a crime chillingly similar to what appeared to have happened in her parents' house.

The victim's name was Bill Frazier and the woman missing was his wife, Joanna. According to the article a son, Riley, survived Bill Frazier.

What had happened to Riley's mother, Joanna? Had she been found and had she been guilty of the murder of his father?

She needed to talk to Riley Frazier. She needed to find out how things had turned out in this case. And she needed to know what it might have to do with her family's case.

Chapter 3

He'd hoped she would call, but he really hadn't been expecting her call so soon. Riley sat in the ice cream parlor that was the bottom floor of the Redbud Bed and Breakfast in the center square of Cherokee Corners.

He was early. She'd told him to meet her here at seven, and it was only now just a little after six. But he'd decided to come early. He'd ordered a cup of coffee, taken a chair facing the door and now waited for Savannah Tallfeather to join him.

She hadn't mentioned the news clipping in her call, only that she'd like to meet with him. He sipped his coffee, watching the people who came and went as he waited.

The ice cream parlor was a popular place. He wondered if it was always so busy or if Saturday nights brought families out for ice cream. Certainly it was ice cream weather—hot and dry like only Oklahoma could be at this time of year.

The front page of the evening edition of the Cherokee Corners newspaper had been filled with the crime that had taken place the night before at the James ranch. Along with the facts that Thomas James was in critical but stable condition and Rita Birdsong James was missing, the article also was a tribute to the couple's contributions to the city.

Thomas James had served as chief of police for ten years, and before that had been on the force for twenty years. During his career he'd received a variety of awards, and recognitions of honor.

His wife, Rita Birdsong James, was no less visible in the community. A full-blooded Cherokee, she was the driving force behind the Cherokee Cultural Center. Her goal had been to educate through entertainment and re-creations of the Cherokee past and present. Both were described as pillars of the community.

Riley's parents hadn't been community icons to anyone but him. His father had been a simple man, a carpenter, and his mother had been a housewife who loved to crochet. In the evenings they had often worked on jigsaw puzzles together.

Two couples, seemingly very different, and yet they both had suffered a similar fate. The pain he felt when he thought of his parents had lessened somewhat with time, but it certainly hadn't gone away.

The most difficult part was that there had been no closure. Sure, the police had closed the file, branded his mother a murderer on the run. But he knew better. He knew that somewhere the real killer of his father ran free and the fate of his mother had yet to be learned.

He'd just finished his first cup of coffee when Savannah walked in. Her gaze locked with his, and in that instant he felt a connection like none he'd ever felt before.

He saw the confusion, the pain in her eyes, felt it resonate with aching familiarity inside him. He was certain it was the connection of two survivors, of two people whose lives had been turned upside down by violent, senseless crime.

His impulse was to stand and draw her into his arms, hold her tight to take away the chill that he knew wrapped tightly around her heart.

But, of course he didn't act on his impulse. She was a virtual stranger, and the last thing he wanted to do was alienate her right from the get-go. He stood as she approached his table. "Officer Tallfeather," he said in greeting.

"Please, make it Savannah," she said, and waved him back into his chair. "I'll be with you in just a minute." She walked over to the counter and greeted the woman working there. The two hugged and spoke for a minute or two, then Savannah returned to the table and sat across from him. "My cousin," she explained.

Before she could say anything else, her cousin appeared at their table. She placed a coffee mug before Savannah, then filled both Savannah's and Riley's cups.

"Alyssa, this is Riley Frazier," Savannah said. "Riley, my cousin, Alyssa Whitefeather."

Alyssa's eyes were as dark and as filled with pain as Savannah's. "Nice to meet you," she murmured in a soft, low voice.

"Nice to meet you, too," Riley replied. "I'm sorry for the pain your family is experiencing right now."

She nodded, then touched Savannah's shoulder. "Let me know if I can get you anything else."

"Thanks, Alyssa," Savannah said.

Once again Savannah directed her gaze at him as Alyssa left the table. She wrapped her long, slender fingers around the coffee cup as if seeking warmth. "I read the newspaper article you gave me," she began.

"I figured you had when you called."

She took a sip of her coffee. "Tell me about it. Tell me about the night it happened."

Riley leaned back in his chair, for a moment rebelling at the thought of revisiting that horrible night. And yet he'd known she'd want him to tell her about it. He'd known when he'd given her that news clipping that he would have to call up everything about that night.

"Before I tell you what happened to them, let me tell you about my parents…about what kind of people they were."

"All right," she agreed.

"They were quiet people and lived an uncomplicated life. My father was a carpenter, my mother a homemaker. He liked to putter in his garden in his spare time and my mother loved to cook and crochet. In the evenings they'd either watch old movies together or work on jigsaw puzzles that they set up on a card table in the living room.''

"You were close to them.'' Her voice was as unemotional as her beautiful features, but her eyes spoke volumes, radiating with pain. He just didn't know if the pain was for him or for herself or perhaps a combination of both.

"I was their only child and yes, I was close to them.'' He thought of the nights when his choice had been to go to the local honky-tonk or spend the evening at his parents' house. He'd often chosen his parents' company. "They were good people.''

"So, what happened...that night?'' The words came from her in hesitation, as if she was sorry to have to ask him such a question.

He raked a hand across his lower jaw and forced himself to go back to that night. "I'd been over to their house that afternoon to show my dad some blueprints of new homes. I had a six-o'clock appointment with clients and so left my folks' place about five-thirty.''

He paused to take a drink of his coffee and felt himself plunging back in time, pulled back into the nightmare. "It was after eight when the clients left, and I realized I'd left some of the blueprints at my folks' house, so I drove back there.''

On one of the walls of the restaurant was a beautiful painting of a redbud tree in bloom. He stared at the picture as he continued. "The front door was open, which really wasn't unusual. I walked into the living room and my father was on the floor in front of his chair. I knew in an instant he was dead."

Grief, as rich and raw as the moment it had happened, seared through him. He cleared his throat. "I picked up the phone and called for help, then went in search of my mother, certain that I'd find her dead, as well."

"But she wasn't there?" Savannah leaned forward, her eyes more alive than before.

"A suitcase was missing, along with some of her clothing, and she immediately was placed at the top of a very short list of suspects." It was impossible for him to keep the edge of bitterness from his voice as he remembered how he'd fought with the police, begging them to look for another killer. "I was also placed on the top of the list, but only for a brief time."

"Your appointment was your alibi?" she asked.

He nodded. "That and the fact that when I left my parents' place that evening both my mom and dad walked me to my car. One of the neighbors was outside and was able to verify that when I left the house my parents were alive and well."

"That was two years ago. What did you find out about your mother? How does the case stand now?" She flushed, her cinnamon skin turning a deeper shade of red. "I mean, I'm sorry for what happened to your father."

He smiled, hoping by the gesture he let her know there was nothing to apologize for, that he understood the reason for the questions before she offered any sympathy. His smile faded as he continued to look at her.

"My mother has never been found." He didn't mean the words to sound as stark as they had. Her eyes widened with surprise.

"And your father's case?" she asked softly.

"Is officially closed. The local authorities are certain my mother is responsible and probably fled the country."

Once again her fingers curled around her mug. "And what do you think?"

This time it was he who leaned forward and held her gaze intently. "I *know* my mother had nothing to do with my father's death. I know it with all my heart, with all my soul, and nothing and nobody will ever make me believe otherwise. If there's anything in this world I'm dead certain of, it's that."

He frowned and leaned back in his chair, realizing he'd become loud and had drawn the attention of the other patrons. "Sorry, I didn't mean to get carried away."

"Please, don't apologize," she replied. "I feel exactly the same way about my mother."

There was more life in her eyes now, a flash of determination Riley could easily identify with. "Are they already saying your mother is a suspect?"

"Yeah. At the moment that's what the evidence points to, and the police will follow the evidence."

She stared down into her coffee cup for a long moment.

He remained silent, giving her time to deal with whatever emotions might be reeling through her. She looked utterly vulnerable with her eyes downcast, displaying the long length of her dark lashes.

She had delicate features, a slender neck and small bones. He'd noticed her scent when she'd first sat down, a fragrance that reminded him of spring days and full-blooming flowers.

How long had it been since he'd noticed the smell of a woman? How long since he'd noticed the curve of a slender neck, the delicacy of feminine hands, the thrust of shapely breasts?

It had been since Patsy. Too long. Something long dormant inside him stirred as he sat watching her, smelling her fresh, feminine scent.

Finally she looked up, her eyes the rich brown of deep chocolate. ''What do you think happened to your mother, Riley?''

A sharp shaft of pain drove through him, banishing the momentary warmth that had filled him. ''I really don't know. Over the past twenty-two months I've come up with hundreds of possibilities, each one more outrageous than the last. She got hit over the head and is wandering around somewhere with no memory of who she is. She became part of the witness-protection program and had to build a new life for herself.''

He flashed her a wry grin. ''Hell, one night I got desperate enough, drunk enough that I checked to make sure there hadn't been any UFO sightings on the night she disappeared. I thought maybe she'd been sucked up into a spaceship as an example of a human being with a perfect heart and soul.''

To his surprise, she reached across the table and placed her hand over his. Her skin was warm. "I'm so sorry for you. It must be horrible—the not knowing.'' She drew her hand back as if suddenly self-conscious. A fierce determination swept over her features. "But I'm sure my mother is going to turn up anytime now. It's all just been a mistake, a terrible misunderstanding of some sort.''

He didn't try to contradict her. He knew how desperately she was clinging to that certainty at the moment. And he hoped she was right. He hoped it all was a terrible misunderstanding and Rita Birdsong James would be found safe and sound and innocent of the charge of attempting to kill her husband.

Savannah took another sip of her coffee, her thoughts racing. Cop thoughts and woman thoughts battled inside her. The crime that had occurred to his family was remarkably similar to what appeared to have happened to hers. Did he have any idea the power of his hypnotic blue eyes?

Was the connection she felt to him that of two people whose lives had been touched by violence, or was she drawn to him because he stirred something inside her that reminded her that she was not just a cop, not just a victim, but a woman as well?

This thought irritated her, and she averted her gaze

from him. Brown eyes, that's what she had loved.
Eyes the color of her own, filled with laughter, filled
with love, that's what she had lost.

"Did the police attempt to find your mother?" she
asked, grasping at the cop inside her rather than the
lonely woman. "Usually when somebody disappears
there's a paper trail of some kind."

He nodded and she couldn't help but notice the rich
shine of his dark-brown hair beneath the artificial
lights overhead. "The authorities checked for activity
on their bank account and credit cards, but there has
been none in the nearly two years since it happened."

She shoved her half-empty cup aside. "There's no
way to ignore the similarities in the two incidents,"
she said.

"That's why I thought it was important I make
contact with you last night. Scott called me as soon
as he heard the first report over his scanner, and that
report indicated a man attacked in his living room and
his wife missing. Scott thought I'd be interested since
it seemed so much like what had happened to my
family."

"But, despite the similarities, it's possible one has
nothing to do with the other," she added hurriedly.
She couldn't imagine her mother missing for two
years. Savannah couldn't stand the thought of not
knowing where her mother was for another two
minutes.

"I'd guess that it's far too early in your investigation to draw any kind of conclusions," he agreed.
"But if you're interested, I have copies of all the

records pertaining to the crime against my parents. I've got witness lists, detective notes, everything.''

She raised an eyebrow in surprise. Family members rarely saw those kinds of things.

"I had a friend on the Sycamore Ridge police force," he said in answer to her unspoken question. "Anyway, you're welcome to see anything I have. Of course, nothing I have will help if it's not the same kind of thing."

"I appreciate the offer," she said. "But I really don't think it would help much." She didn't want to believe there was any connection between what had happened to his family and what had happened to hers. After all, his father had died and his mother had never been found.

Suddenly she wanted to be away from him, needed to be away from him. It was almost as if she felt that if she spent too much time here with him, his tragedy would become her own.

"Thank you so much for meeting with me," she said, and rose from her chair.

"No problem." He got up, as well. He was taller than she remembered from the night before—tall with broad shoulders and slender hips. It was the physique of a man who worked a job of physical labor. He began to pull his wallet from his back pocket, but she waved her hand.

"Please, the coffee is on me."

She was grateful he didn't try to fight her for it. She was far too tired, far too emotionally fragile to fight over something as inconsequential as a dollar cup of coffee.

"Thanks for the coffee," he said as he walked to the door of the shop.

"Thanks for the information," she replied. Together they stepped outside, where night had fallen and the surrounding stores had closed up for the night. The night brought with it a terrifying sense of loss as she realized that her mother had been missing for nearly twenty-four hours.

"Your father...is he doing all right?"

"He's hanging in there. He's a stubborn Irishman with a hard head."

He quirked a dark brow upward. "Irish, huh? I would have never guessed. You and your sister and brother don't look Irish."

"My father always teased that Mom wasn't happy unless she dominated everything, including the gene pool." She swallowed hard as a wave of emotion swept over her. "It was nice meeting you, Riley," she said, and held her hand out to him.

"I wish it had been under different circumstances." He reached for her hand, but to her surprise instead pulled her into an awkward hug. "I'm so sorry about your family," he said into her hair. "I hope...I pray that everything turns out okay." He released her as quickly as he'd hugged her, then murmured a good-night and walked away.

She stood on the sidewalk, shell-shocked, a bundle of exposed nerves and heightened sensations. It had been a very long time since she'd felt the press of a muscular chest against hers, the warmth of strong arms surrounding her. In the instant that he'd hugged her, she'd smelled him, a distinctly woodsy male scent that was quite appealing. Too appealing.

She turned and went back into the ice cream parlor. She joined her cousin Alyssa behind the counter where she was making a fresh pot of coffee. Alyssa finished what she was doing then turned and embraced Savannah. "Is there any news?"

Savannah shook her head. "I spoke with Bree before coming here and there's no change in Dad's condition. Clay is trying to get Glen to let him into the house or at least see what the crime scene has gathered so far, but Glen is refusing."

Alyssa sank down on a stool. "This is what I saw," she said softly. "I knew something bad was coming…knew somebody was going to be hurt…but I couldn't tell who…I couldn't stop it." Tears filled her eyes, threatening to spill down her cheeks.

"Melinda, keep an eye on things, okay?" Savannah asked the young woman who worked for Alyssa. Savannah took Alyssa by the arm and pulled her through the doorway that led to Alyssa's living quarters.

She closed the door behind them, shutting off the sounds from the ice cream parlor and led Alyssa to the cream-colored sofa where they sat side by side. She took Alyssa's hands in hers and squeezed tightly.

"Alyssa, everyone in the family knows how your visions come to you. We all know that most of the time you can't figure out exactly what they mean. Nobody blames you for not seeing this coming.''

''I know that, but it's just so frustrating,'' she replied. She pulled her hands from Savannah's grasp and used one to push a strand of her long dark hair behind an ear. ''Over the past two months, I've had a single, recurring vision, and it's been different from any other one I've ever had.''

Although Savannah had heard this before, she sat patiently and listened, knowing Alyssa needed to talk about it. ''What I've experienced over the past two months weren't even real visions,'' Alyssa continued, her eyes dark and worried. ''There was never a picture…just a feeling of horrible doom, of enormous grief and emptiness. Is there any news on Aunt Rita?''

''None.''

Alyssa frowned. ''I had a new vision this morning…about Aunt Rita.''

Savannah leaned toward her cousin, her heartbeat quickening with hope. Maybe Alyssa's newest vision could provide a clue of some kind as to where Rita was…what had happened to her. ''What? What did you see?''

Alyssa frowned, a delicate furrow appearing across her brow. ''It won't help,'' she said as if reading Savannah's thoughts. ''It doesn't make any sense.''

''Tell me anyway,'' Savannah replied.

''I saw Aunt Rita in bed. She was sleeping peacefully in her own bed, in her own room.'' She sighed in frustration. ''I told you it wouldn't help.''

Savannah frowned thoughtfully. "Are you sure it was her own bed?"

"Positive. I saw her beneath the dark-blue floral bedspread that's on their bed. I saw the Tiffany-style lamp they have on the nightstand. It was her room, Savannah. I told you it wouldn't help. We both know Aunt Rita isn't safe and sound and sleeping in her bed at home."

Savannah reached for her cousin's hand once again. From the time they had all been children together, the James siblings had known that their favorite cousin had mysterious visions. The visions were as much a part of Alyssa as her long, dark hair and gentle nature.

"But you'll tell me if you have any more visions of her?" Savannah asked.

"Of course," Alyssa replied.

"Even if they seem crazy or unimportant?"

Alyssa's lips curved into a half smile. "Even then."

"And if you think you see anything that might help find her, you have to promise me you'll tell Chief Cleberg."

The half smile fell into a frown. "Glen Cleberg is like nine-tenths of the people in this town. They all think I'm more than a little crazy."

"I know the chief has given you a hard time before when you've tried to help, but you've got to promise me you'll tell him if you see anything that might help us find Mom."

"I promise," she agreed. "You know I'll do whatever I can to help find her. She's always been like a mother to me.'' Tears once again sprang to Alyssa's eyes, and she and Savannah hugged.

Alyssa's mother had died when Alyssa was four, and it had been Rita who had stepped in to fill the empty space in the little girl's life.

''Who is Riley Frazier?'' Alyssa asked as Savannah stood.

''A man who had something horrible happen to his parents a couple of years ago. He was offering me his support.''

''Nice-looking man,'' Alyssa said, also rising from the sofa.

Savannah shrugged. ''I guess.'' A vision of Riley streaked through her mind. ''I've got to get going. I want to stop by the hospital on my way home.''

Alyssa walked with her to the door. ''You doing okay?'' she asked.

''I'm holding up,'' Savannah replied.

Alyssa gazed at her with warm affection. ''You were always the strong one, Savannah. I've always admired your incredible wealth of strength.''

Alyssa's words replayed in her head thirty minutes later as she sat by her father's hospital bed.

The sight of her father lying there, so pale, so lifeless had shocked her. Thomas James was a big man with an even bigger presence. Now, with his head wrapped in bandages and his mouth hanging slack, hooked up to a variety of monitors and machines and with deep, dark circles beneath his eyes, he looked frighteningly old and fragile.

Savannah took his hand in hers. Cold...his hand

was so cold. Tears welled up in her eyes as she gazed at him. "Daddy," she said softly. Did he hear her? Could he hear her? "Daddy, you need to wake up." She squeezed his hand. "We need you…I need you."

It was all too much, she thought. Her mother missing, her father in a coma—it was all too much to survive. She released his hand and leaned back in her chair, utterly exhausted both physically and mentally.

Alyssa had been wrong. She wasn't strong. She wasn't strong at all. She wasn't strong enough to survive what had become of her life, nor was she strong enough to let go of the bridge support and join her Jimmy in the spirit world.

She felt as if she was caught in some horrible state of limbo, too cowardly to join her husband in death, but equally afraid to contemplate what lay ahead for herself and the people she loved.

Chapter 4

Every morning when Riley left his house and headed for work, he passed by his parents' house. As the early-morning light played on the neat little ranch house surrounded by trees and bushes, it gave the place a golden aura of warmth. One would never know the house had been the scene of a violent crime.

During the summer months, Riley kept the yard mowed and weeded, and in the winter months he would shovel snow from the driveway and sidewalks. But, since the day the police had released the house back to him, he hadn't been back inside it.

The house was in his name so he could sell it or rent it out if he so chose, but he couldn't. It was here, just the way she'd left it. It was here, waiting for his mother's return.

This morning as he drove past the house, his

thoughts were filled with Savannah Tallfeather and the conversation they'd shared two nights before.

She'd been reluctant to completely acknowledge the unmistakable similarities between his case and hers. He understood her reluctance. If she believed the same perpetrator was responsible not only for what had happened to his family, but to hers, then she also had to accept the possibility that her mother's whereabouts might still be a mystery two years from now.

She wasn't ready to face that possibility.

A swell of pride filled him as he turned off the main road and drove through a stone entrance. Gold lettering on the left side of the entrance read Frazier Estates.

Just ahead was the trailer that had served as Riley's office since he'd begun this dream project four months ago. In the distance he could see the rooftops of the four model homes that were nearing completion.

Pride mingled with a bittersweet pang of grief as he parked in front of the trailer. For so many nights he and his father had sat at the kitchen table and planned this, plotted this, dreamed this, and now the dream was within Riley's hands. But his father wasn't here to share it with him.

He wasn't surprised to see Lillian's car already parked in front of the trailer. He'd hired the sixty-two-year-old woman six months ago as his secretary. However, in the space of those months she'd become a combination of secretary, personal assistant, friend and mother hen. There were times when she could be as annoying as hell, but he positively adored her.

The scent of fresh-brewed coffee greeted him as he entered the trailer. Lillian sat at her desk with the morning paper spread out before her.

"Morning, Lillian."

"Morning, boss. Coffee is made and there are some muffins on the counter…bran. You should eat a couple. You young people don't get enough fiber in your diet."

"Fiber isn't high on my priority list, Lillian," he said wryly.

She quirked upward a perfectly plucked silver eyebrow. "Wait until you get to be my age, then fiber intake definitely becomes a priority."

Riley poured himself a cup of coffee, then grabbed one of the muffins from the flowered plate. "I'll eat a muffin, okay?" he said as he disappeared into his office.

The day was the usual blend of headaches and happiness: supplies arrived late; a fistfight erupted between two roofers; his foreman threatened to quit for the fifth time in as many days…they were the usual headaches that came with a big construction job.

The tension headache he'd begun to nurse by ten vanished at eleven when a young, newlywed couple stopped by to have a look around.

As he showed them the plans for the community he envisioned and saw their excitement and interest, he was the happiest he'd been in years.

In between the headaches and the joys the day

brought, thoughts of Savannah intruded at odd moments. As he watched the hardwood floors in one of the model homes being varnished, he thought of her skin. A lot of women would pay a lot of money to get that beautiful cinnamon shade of her skin.

He thought of the moment when he'd told her goodbye, and spontaneously pulled her into a hug. She had been neither a willing nor unwilling participant in the embrace. It had been rather like hugging an inanimate, unemotional stuffed animal.

Eventually her numbness would wear off, he thought. And then the grief would begin in earnest. But she wasn't a stranger to grief. She'd lost her husband a year before.

At noon he ordered a pizza to be delivered from the local pizzeria. Lillian would give him hell about his food choices, but he'd become a junk-food junkie in the past couple of months.

He'd just hung up the phone from ordering the pizza when it rang. He grabbed it up and murmured a hello.

"Riley?"

He recognized her voice immediately. The low, dulcet tones sent a wave of warmth through him. "Hi, Savannah."

"I'm sorry to bother you, but I was wondering…about those papers…those files you have from two years ago…" Her voice trailed off, as if she was reluctant to come right out and ask him for what she wanted.

"Would you like to take a look at them?"

"If you wouldn't mind."

"Not at all. Just tell me when and where."

"Have you eaten lunch yet?" she asked.

He thought of the pizza he'd just ordered…easy come, easy go. "No."

"Could you get away for a little while now?" Her voice was hesitant, as if she was afraid of asking too much of him.

"Sure," he agreed easily. "Savannah, I know what you're going through. Whatever I can do to help, just tell me."

"Could you meet me in an hour? How about at the Briarwood Truck Stop. We could have lunch while I go over the paperwork."

"Fine. I'll see you there in an hour." Riley hung up the phone and immediately got up from his desk. The Briarwood Truck Stop wasn't the snazziest place in the world, but it was located between Sycamore Ridge and Cherokee Corners. It would be about a half hour drive for both of them.

Before meeting her he'd have to go back to his house and grab the file that held all the paperwork that had been generated in the case of his father's homicide.

"There's a pepperoni pizza coming in about twenty minutes," he said to Lillian. He threw a twenty on her desk. "Enjoy the pizza and I'll be unreachable for the rest of the afternoon."

"Wait…you've got an appointment at two with Hal Brooks from Brooks Carpeting."

"Cancel it. Set something up with him for tomorrow," he said as he flew out the trailer door.

It was ridiculous how much he looked forward to seeing her again he thought as he drove to his home to get the files. It was ridiculous that his heart was racing just a little bit faster since her call.

He told himself it was nothing more than a continuation of the strange connection he'd felt when he'd first seen her...the connection of two survivors.

He told himself that his eagerness to see her again was because maybe, just maybe, something he found out about what had happened to her parents would bring him some closure as to what had happened to his.

But, even as he told himself all these things, he knew it was more than that. Part of the connection he'd felt had been one as old as time—the response of a male to an attractive female.

It had been years since he'd felt that charge of adrenaline, the rush of possibility where a woman was concerned.

He'd thought he'd found the perfect woman three years before. Patsy Gerrard had been attractive, witty and charming, and they had dated for just a little over a year. Their relationship had been one of the casualties of crime.

During those nightmare days immediately following his father's death and his mother's disappearance, he'd discovered that witty could be shallow, that charming could grate and what felt right through the good times often became terribly wrong during bad times.

It had been a relief when Patsy had moved on and he could give himself solely to the grief of losing his parents. But now he realized he'd been alone for too long, focused too intensely on his work and fighting loneliness during quiet moments to himself.

He pulled up in the driveway of his beautiful story-and-a-half home. The house had been his first building project and thankfully had been completed before the night of the crime.

His mother had fussed that the place was too big, too sterile for her son, and his father had explained that since Riley was a builder the house where he lived was important for future business. He'd assured his wife that it wouldn't be long before Riley would have the house filled with things to make it warm and homey. Riley knew his mother was hoping he'd find a wife to warm up the house.

It was still a cold and sterile place, Riley thought as he ran into his study and grabbed the thick file from his file cabinet. Since his father's death and his mother's disappearance, he'd done little to make the place a home. Maybe it was time, he thought.

Minutes later, as he drove to the Briarwood Truck Stop, he reminded himself that Savannah was in no position to be interested in pursuing any kind of relationship with a man. Her world had been turned upside down, her mother was missing and her father was still in a coma. The last thing on her mind would be romance.

But she could use a friend, he thought. And what better friend than a person who'd already been through the same kinds of things she was experiencing? What better friend than a man seeking answers to the same kinds of questions she had?

Savannah sat in one of the red leather booths in the Briarwood Truck Stop, toying with the silverware as she waited for Riley to arrive.

She'd hesitated before calling him, stewing it over for a full day before succumbing to desperation. It had now been almost ninety-six hours since her father had been hurt and her mother had disappeared.

Although she and her brother and sister were being kept out of the investigation loop, she knew that it had stalled and was going nowhere.

She sighed and motioned to the waitress for a refill on her coffee. She'd been living on coffee for the past three days, coffee and nerves. She'd just finished her second cup when he entered the restaurant.

Her pulse quickened slightly at the sight of him. Clad in a pair of navy dress slacks and a navy-and-white-striped dress shirt, he looked every inch a successful businessman. But as he walked toward her, she noted that he had an aura of strength, of power about him. It seemed obvious to her that he was a man confident of who he was, a man more than capable of taking care of himself.

He carried in one hand a bulky manila file and her heartbeat raced as she anticipated looking at what was inside. Since she couldn't investigate the crime that had occurred in her parents' home, she was eager to look through the files detailing the crime that had occurred in Riley's parents' home.

At least it was something to do, she thought. Glen had kept her away from work, and she had nothing to do except wait for her mother to return and wait for her father to come out of his coma. The waiting, she feared, would make her go more than a little crazy.

Looking through Riley's files might be nothing more than a dead end, but at least it was something for her to do beside sitting idle and thinking.

"Savannah." His gaze was warm as he greeted her. He slid into the booth across from her and shoved the folder to the side of the table. "I heard there's been no change in your father's condition and you haven't heard anything about your mother. How are you holding up?"

"Okay, I guess." Her gaze shot to the folder.

He placed a hand over it and smiled gently at her. "We eat first, then you can look through it."

"I'm really not hungry," she replied.

"But you have to eat," he returned. She looked at him with a touch of irritation. She didn't need a virtual stranger telling her what to do, and she certainly didn't need a mother figure.

Again he smiled, as if he knew exactly what she was thinking. "I've been there, Savannah. I know how slowly the hours can creep by while you wait for answers that make sense. I know how hard it is to sleep, how the simple act of eating doesn't seem important. But you have to keep your strength up. Your father is going to need you when he comes out of his coma and your mother is going to need you when she comes back home.''

Before she could reply, the waitress appeared at their table. ''I'd like a cheeseburger, fries and a soda,'' he said, then looked at Savannah expectantly.

His little lecture had made sense and she opened the menu and frowned at it, trying to find something that would whet her appetite, but nothing sounded the least bit appetizing. Aware of Riley's gaze on her, she closed the menu. ''I'll just have the soup of the day and a dinner roll.''

The waitress left, and for a moment the two of them sat in silence. As she had the last time she'd met him, she smelled his scent…clean male coupled with woodsy cologne. ''Are you married, Riley?'' The question surprised her. It had fallen from her lips before becoming a conscious thought in her mind.

''No. Got close once, but then the thing with my folks sort of broke us apart.''

''Oh, I'm sorry.''

He waved a hand and grinned. ''Don't be. The biggest mistake I would ever have made in my life would have been to marry Patsy. The messiness of the crime and the fallout from my emotional craziness was just too much for her to handle. She likes things neat and tidy, and there was nothing neat and tidy about me or the situation. I'm just grateful I found out before we got married instead of after.''

"Your emotional craziness…what does that mean?" she asked curiously.

"Probably what you're going through right now."

"I'm not going through anything," she said.

He lifted a dark eyebrow wryly and leaned forward. "Then, you aren't having problems concentrating? You aren't having to talk around a ball of emotion so thick in your throat it threatens to suffocate you? The little minutia of life isn't ticking you off…the laughter of strangers, the birds' chirping, the need to pay bills?"

Initially his words offended her. She felt violated, as if he'd looked into her heart, seen the anguish of her soul. Then she realized he had, in a way. He'd been through it—the pain, the uncertainty, the anger that seemed to exclude everything else in her life since the moment she'd arrived at her parents' home that night.

"You're right," she finally replied, her voice flat and hollow to her own ears. "The woman where I got my gas earlier today told me good morning, and I had the sudden urge to reach across the counter and slap her silly."

She shook her head ruefully. "I want to scream and I want to cry, and more than anything I want it all to just go away. I want my father to wake up and my mom to come back and things to go back to the way they were."

She drew a deep breath, surprised by her own outburst. "I'm sorry…I just…nobody else seems to understand what I'm going through.'' She stared down at the tabletop, unable to meet his gaze.

''What about your sister and brother? Surely they're going through the same things that you are. Are the three of you close?''

''We're close, but Breanna just got married and has her husband, Adam. Clay—'' she frowned, then continued ''—Clay is so angry right now he's not letting anyone get close to him. He's a crime-scene investigator and it's killing him that nobody will let him into the house to do his job.''

He covered her hand with his own. ''So, when you feel all alone and have nobody to talk to about the emotional crazies, don't hesitate to call on me. You need to have somebody who understands what you're going through.''

His hand was warm, his palm callused and strong over hers, and it felt good, which made her pull her hand away. His offer of support filled her with warmth. ''And just who did you have who understood what you were going through? From what you told me a moment ago, Patsy didn't. And didn't you tell me before that you're an only child?''

He leaned back against the leather booth. ''Yeah, it was just me.'' His blue eyes darkened to the deep shade of midnight. ''I didn't have anyone to help me through it and I have to tell you there were times I wasn't sure I was going to survive it.''

''How did you survive it?''

''I'm still surviving it,'' he replied. ''It isn't as difficult as it was initially, but it's still with me...the questions, the uncertainty.'' He stopped talking as the waitress arrived at their table with their orders.

''I have kind of a rule about dining,'' he said when the waitress had left once again.

''And what's that?'' The darkness in his eyes had left, and again she was struck by the beautiful blue of his eyes. She'd thought that was his appeal, what made him appear so handsome. But sitting across from him, she realized the startling color of his eyes was only part of it.

He had a firm, square chin that spoke of strong convictions and perhaps a bit of stubbornness. When he looked at her there was an attentiveness in his gaze that was both engaging and slightly provocative.

His dark hair had just enough curl and not quite enough style to keep it from falling over his broad forehead. His face and forearms were tanned, indicating a man who spent a lot of time outdoors.

''The rule is that we talk of nothing unpleasant while we eat. Unpleasantness at mealtime causes ulcers.''

''Is that a medical certainty?''

He grinned, exposing his straight white teeth in a charming fashion. ''That's a mother certainty. It was my mother's most strict rule and I still honor it.''

''Okay,'' she agreed, and looked with disinterest down at her bowl of soup. It was minestrone, and nothing had ever looked less appetizing.

The silence between them stretched out and she felt the weight of it pressing against her chest. She felt as if she should say something, make some sort of meaningless small talk, but she seemed to have lost the ability.

She grabbed her dinner roll and pulled it apart and shot a surreptitious glance at Riley. He caught the glance and smiled sympathetically as if he knew idle conversation was beyond her grasp.

"It must be interesting, your work as a homicide detective," he said.

She eyed him wryly. "If the conversation is supposed to be pleasant, then it's not a great idea for me to talk about my work."

"Ah, just the opening I was waiting for. Now I get to tell you about my work." Again his charming smile. "You know how men love to talk about themselves."

The burst of laughter that escaped her lips both surprised and appalled her. How could she laugh—about anything—with the situation with her parents? The laughter died on a burst of guilt and tears suddenly stung her eyes. She stared down, fighting to get her emotions under control.

"It's all right, Savannah," he said softly. "Even though something bad has happened in your life, you've got to laugh when you get the chance. God knows it can't hurt your parents."

"Logically I know that," she exclaimed.

"Trust me, I know that you can't maintain the grief every moment of every day. It makes you a difficult person to be around." He gestured toward her soup bowl.

"Were you difficult to be around?" Dutifully, she picked up her spoon and took a sip of the soup.

He popped a French fry into his mouth and nodded. "I still have difficult days."

For the next few minutes they focused on their meals. To Savannah's surprise, the soup was quite good and awakened a hunger she hadn't realized she possessed.

"You haven't really taken the opportunity to talk about yourself," she observed as she buttered her dinner roll.

He'd nearly finished his cheeseburger and he took a sip of his soda before answering. "I decided to be kind and not bore you."

She had a feeling he was many things, but boring wasn't one of them. "Consider this an invitation to bore me."

He smiled, and again she was struck by the force of his appeal. "As you probably know from looking at my business card, I'm a builder. This spring we broke ground on my biggest project to date...my dream, really."

"And what's that?" She was always interested in hearing about other people's dreams, especially since she'd lost all of hers.

"Riley Estates," he said as if those two words explained everything.

"A development," she replied.

"More than just a development." His eyes lit with life. "It's going to be a community with amenities for everyone from the very young to the very old.

Along with the new homes, I've agreed to refurbish some of the stores in downtown Sycamore Ridge to induce merchants back.''

"Sounds like a big job all the way around," she observed.

"It is, but I'm hoping Riley Estates will bring people, and with people more stores will open and Sycamore Ridge will become the thriving little metropolis it once was.''

"You grew up in Sycamore Ridge?''

"Born and raised there.''

"Savannah?''

The deep, familiar voice came from somewhere behind her. She turned, then scooted out of the bench and hugged the distinguished-looking older man who stood near their booth. "Jacob! What are you doing here?''

"I was on my way home from one of the branch offices and thought I'd stop in here and grab a bite to eat." He squeezed her hands in his. "I can't begin to tell you how upset I've been over this thing with your mother and father. Has there been any news today?''

"None," she said as he released her hands.

"I'm offering a twenty-five thousand dollar reward to anyone with information about the whereabouts of your mother or whomever hurt your father.''

"You don't have to do that," Savannah protested faintly.

His pale blue eyes radiated a combination of pain and concern. "I have to do something. Your parents were two of my dearest friends. I'm not good with anything but money.''

Savannah hugged the portly man. "Thank you.''

He looked at his watch. "I've got to run. I have an afternoon appointment to get to.''

As he left, Savannah slid back into the booth and instantly realized she'd been rude. "I'm sorry, I should have introduced you," she said to Riley. "I wasn't thinking.''

"It's all right. I recognized him. Jacob Kincaid, owner of Kincaid Banks.''

"And a close friend of my parents. He's putting up a large reward for information about my mother and father.''

"That's nice.''

She shrugged. "We'll see. It's been my experience that rewards tend to bring out every nutcase in the county. Glen won't be overly pleased. A reward usually means more work for the people working the case. But it also sometimes takes just one tip to crack a case wide open.'' She eyed the manila folder he'd brought with him. "Would you mind if I took that with me?''

"Actually, I would." His gaze held an unspoken apology. "I didn't think to make copies before I left home, and I'd prefer it not leave my possession. My cop buddy left the force and if anything were to happen to these reports, I'd never be able to get copies again. You can look through them now, or if you'd prefer you can read through them at my place or yours. The other alternative is that you can get copies as soon as I have some made.''

She didn't want to wait, but she hadn't really thought it through when she'd asked him to meet her here. She didn't feel comfortable reading the files now…here in a public place.

''If you don't mind…maybe you could follow me to my place,'' she said. ''I really don't feel like we should go through it all here.''

''I agree, and I don't mind at all following you.''

Fifteen minutes later Savannah was regretting inviting him to her place. She should have just looked through the file at the truck stop.

She clenched the steering wheel tightly and glanced in the rearview mirror where Riley's pickup was visible. He was nice…too nice. He was attractive…too attractive.

''Don't worry, Jimmy,'' she whispered aloud. ''No man, no matter how nice, no matter how attractive, will ever take your place in my heart, in my soul.''

It was about the crime and nothing more. The crime they both had suffered explained the attraction she felt for Riley Frazier.

Once she read through his reports and files concerning the crime against his parents, then she would be done with him. Her heart would still belong to the man who'd been her soul mate from the time they'd been children.

Chapter 5

Riley thought he had no preconceptions about where Savannah lived. Still, he was vaguely surprised when she pulled into an attractive apartment complex and parked. He realized that somewhere in the back of his mind he'd assumed she was a house kind of person.

He followed her up the sidewalk to her unit, the manila folder clutched tightly in his hand.

He was glad she hadn't wanted to go over the file in the truck stop. Even though he'd read the reports a hundred times in the past two years, he still wasn't inured to the emotional assault he felt when looking at them.

"Come on in," she said as she opened the door.

"Thanks." He entered ahead of her into a small foyer. The focal point was a beautiful oil painting of bears in the wilderness. "Gorgeous art," he said.

''It's the work of a local artist. Her name is Tamara Greystone. She teaches school and paints in her spare time. Let's go into the kitchen. I'll put on a pot of coffee.''

''Sounds good.''

She led him through a nice-size living room decorated in earth tones. The first things that snagged his attention were the photographs. They littered the room—small ones, larger ones, all framed and all of the same man.

He wasn't a particularly handsome man. Obviously Native American, his nose was a bit large and hooked, and his face was slightly chubby. But something about his eyes and his wide smile in each of the photos radiated an innate warmth and friendliness.

It wasn't so much a living room as a shrine to the man Riley presumed had been her husband. There were also photos of him and her together. In each of those her hair was long and her face held a bright, happy smile that made his heart ache for her loss.

''I heard about your husband,'' he said, aware that she'd seen him looking at the photos. ''I'm sorry.''

''Thank you.'' Her lips pressed tightly together, indicating to him that she intended to say nothing more on the subject.

The kitchen was bright and airy, decorated in an apple motif and smelling faintly of cinnamon. Windows surrounded a round oak table on three sides, giving an open, airy feel to the room. She gestured him to a chair at the table while she opened a cabinet and began to prepare the coffee.

"This is nice," he said. "How long have you been here?"

"I moved in about six months ago. Do you take cream or sugar in your coffee?"

"No, thanks. Black is fine." So, she'd moved in here after her husband had died. Probably escaping memories. A new burst of compassion for her swept through him. He'd lost his parents, and although it had been intensely painful, it couldn't compare to losing a spouse.

As the kitchen filled with the scent of the fresh-brewed coffee, she pulled cups out of the cabinet and placed them on the table as Riley struggled to come up with some benign conversational topic.

"It's sure warm for so early in the summer," he finally said.

She shot him a quicksilver smile that lit up her features and nearly stole his breath away. "When uncertain about making conversation the safe resort is always the weather."

The smile was only there a moment, then gone, making him feel oddly bereft. "I was just making idle chatter," he replied.

She grabbed the coffeepot and filled their cups. "I know. The ability to make small talk seems to have eluded me some time ago." She put the coffeepot away, then joined him at the table.

He shrugged. "The ability to make small talk is vastly overrated. There's nothing wrong with moments of silence occasionally."

"Sometimes, though, too much silence can almost send you over the edge."

"True," he agreed, then took a sip of his coffee. He thought of what she'd said, about too much silence, and wondered how much she'd suffered in the past year since the death of her husband. He wondered if she had any idea how revealing her words had been, that she'd given him an intimate glimpse of her life.

"Well, I guess it's time to get to work." She drew a deep breath, her gaze on the manila folder. He pulled his chair around to the same side of the table where she sat.

"I have to warn you, some of this is kind of graphic," he said.

"Riley, I'm a homicide cop. I've seen graphic plenty of times before."

He opened the file and despite her last words, he heard her soft gasp as she saw the photo of his dead father on the floor next to a buttery tan recliner. Despite the fact that he'd believed himself mentally prepared to see the photo once again, the vision caused his breath to momentarily catch in the back of his throat.

Dad. His head filled with images of his father at the same time his heart cried out in pain.

He cleared his throat. "Apparently he was in his recliner when he was hit from behind with a blunt object. He fell forward and tumbled from the chair to the floor."

"Was the weapon found?"

"No."

"No weapon was found at my parents' house, either." She turned the photo over and picked up the medical examiner's report.

For the next half hour Riley sipped his coffee and watched as she read page after page of reports. He liked looking at her. Her features radiated so many things—strength, yet a soft vulnerability, determination mingling with a hint of stubbornness and an exquisite femininity he found captivating.

Occasionally she would ask him questions, take in his replies, then go back to reading. It was obvious her entire focus was on the reports. That was fine with him. He was content to sit next to her and smell the sweet scent of her, feel the body heat that radiated from her and wonder what it would be like to taste her lips.

It surprised him, that something about her had awakened a hunger that hadn't been present in him for a very long time. Something about her made him think about hot kisses and the sweet hollow between female breasts.

Her hands fascinated him. They were slender, delicate and her fingernails were painted a pearly pink. He couldn't imagine them holding a gun. They seemed much more suited to stroking a brow…or holding a baby.

He frowned, aware that his thoughts were definitely sexist. He'd seen her handle her gun the night she'd drawn it on him in the hospital parking lot. She'd been coolly efficient, as if the gun were a natural extension of her arm.

"I've read all the notes about the people the police interviewed at the time of the incident. It sounds like your parents were very nice people," she said, and looked at him.

"They were." He leaned back in his chair to get a bit of distance from her, aware that his thoughts of moments before still had half possession of his brain. "They were quiet people. They didn't have a wide circle of friends, but they didn't have any enemies, either. I think that's why it was so easy for the officials to assume it was a domestic dispute gone bad."

"Despite the fact that nobody had ever seen signs of marital discord between your mother and father?"

He smiled with a touch of bitterness. "You know what they say, nobody knows what goes on behind closed doors. I guess the cops were able to figure that just because a couple doesn't air their dirty laundry in public doesn't mean there isn't any dirty laundry."

She closed the file, a frown creasing her brow. "In my parents' case it's just the opposite. The authorities don't have to speculate about dirty laundry behind closed doors."

He leaned forward once again. "What do you mean?"

She scooted back from the table and stood, as if uncomfortable with his nearness. She leaned against the cabinets, the frown still furrowing her forehead.

"Half the people in town can attest to the fact that my parents fought and fought often. They were loud and passionate fights, but never physical.'' She smiled, but it was a curious mix of pleasure and pain. ''I think they were two people who were stimulated by the arguments. You know there are people like that.''

He nodded and found himself wondering what her relationship had been like with her husband. Had they been like her parents? Stimulating each other with fights so the make-up sessions would be more exciting and intense? Or had they been more like his parents—quiet with their passion for each other, rarely exchanging words of conflict?

It didn't really matter what kind of relationship she had shared with her husband. It was obvious from the photo display in the living room that their relationship had been a loving one.

He shook his head in an attempt to focus on what she was saying and not on how lovely she looked.

''I really appreciate you letting me see the files,'' she said. ''I'm not sure that anything I read will help in my case, but it was kind of you to share it with me.''

He sensed a dismissal in her words and in the way she crossed her arms over her chest. ''Actually, my reasons for letting you look at them were not altogether altruistic,'' he replied. ''If the same perpetrator is responsible for your crime and mine, then perhaps in helping you to solve yours, I can find out who murdered my father and what happened to my mother.''

''Whatever the reasons, I appreciate it.'' She

moved to the table and gathered up the papers. He knew it was a subtle action to get him on his way.

He reluctantly got to his feet and wasn't surprised when she led him back through the living room and to the front door. He felt a sense of rising panic, knowing that unless something else happened he'd probably never see her again, never talk to her again.

He told himself that he hardly knew her and had contacted her strictly as one victim seeking out another, as somebody hoping to find answers. But his interest in her had quickly outgrown that particular desire.

"Thank you again, Riley," she said at the door and offered him her hand.

He took it, enjoying the feel of its delicate femininity against his harder, bigger hand. "Anything I can do, Savannah, anything at all, don't hesitate to call me." He knew he was holding her hand longer than necessary, but he was reluctant to give it up. "Even if you just need to talk, I'm only a phone call away."

"Thank you." She pulled her hand away and there was nothing more for Riley to say, nothing more for him to do but leave.

As he drove away from the apartment complex, thoughts of her filled his head. He thought again of the pictures he'd seen, the ones where she'd been smiling and there had been no darkness in her eyes, no hint of the profound sadness that darkened them now.

Would she ever find that smile again? That bright,

beautiful smile that lit her features from within? If she ever did, he hoped he'd be around to see it.

''What are you doing here?'' Glen Cleberg greeted Savannah with a scowl as she walked into the brick building that housed the Cherokee Corners Police Department.

''I work here,'' she replied.

''I told you to take some time off,'' he replied.

She set her purse on her desk. ''Glen, it's been over a week. If I don't get back to work, I swear I'll go crazy. Don't make me go back home.''

Glen grabbed her arm and steered her into his private office. He pointed her to the chair in front of his desk as he pulled the door closed behind them.

Savannah steeled herself for a war. She couldn't stand the endless days and nights anymore. She'd spent hours at the hospital watching her motionless father, and hours wandering the streets trying to think of what might have happened to her mother.

''Glen, please don't send me home,'' she said again before he could say anything. ''I need to get back to work. We've still got an open murder case to solve.''

He nodded. ''The Maxwell case…I know.'' He frowned and rubbed his hand across his meaty jaw. ''I can't have you mucking around in your parents' case.'' His frown deepened. ''But, I'll be honest, Savannah, we do need you on the Maxwell thing. You have a better grasp of the case than anyone else working it.''

The case he spoke of was one Gregory Maxwell,

found naked and dead in front of the public library. Savannah had been the first officer on the scene and had been assigned lead investigator. "Anything new on it since I've been out?"

"Nothing." Glen released a puffy sigh of frustration. "And Maxwell was well liked, highly respected. Folks want to know who did such a terrible thing."

"Then let me get back to work," she exclaimed.

He hesitated a long moment and pulled his hand across his lower jaw once again. "Okay." He leaned across his desk and pointed a stubby finger at her. "But you keep your investigation skills focused on the Maxwell case. You don't bother the men working your parents' case. That's not a homicide, and we're keeping you apprised of the details you need to know."

Which was nothing, she thought with a touch of bitterness. It had been eight days and there had been nothing new on the case. Her father was still in his coma and her mother was still missing and Jimmy, her sweet Jimmy was still dead.

"Get out of here and solve the Maxwell case," Glen said. "But your brother is still on paid leave. I don't want him anywhere near the lab until the forensic work is complete on your case."

She didn't waste time arguing with him, afraid that he might change his mind about her coming back to work. Instead she left his office and headed for her desk. She was greeted by fellow officers, most of whom had already given her their regrets over what had happened to her family.

The Maxwell file was on her desk just where she'd left it the last time she'd been in the station. She picked it up and read through her notes, trying to get back into the case that had haunted her before her personal tragedy had struck.

Greg Maxwell had been thirty-two years old at the time of his murder. He'd built a successful business selling and repairing computers and writing computer programs. He'd lived in a lovely home with an equally lovely wife, but somebody had stabbed him, then had undressed him, leaving him naked in the middle of the sidewalk as a final insult.

The authorities had uncovered no financial problems, no secret vices and no marital discord in their investigation.

She studied her notes of her interview with Virginia Maxwell, Greg's wife, but she found her thoughts wandering to Riley.

Long after he'd left her apartment his clean male scent had lingered. Somehow the smell had brought back her grief and thoughts of all she had lost when Jimmy had died.

After showing Riley to the door, she'd returned to the kitchen table and breathed the air that held his scent as she'd drunk yet another cup of coffee. She'd liked the way his hand had felt holding hers. His had been the hands of a working man—strong and competent and slightly rough.

He'd been in her thoughts often in the days since she'd last seen him. She told herself her only interest in him was the fact that he'd been through what she was going through. He was living proof that not knowing the whereabouts of a loved one could be survived.

But somewhere deep inside her, she knew it was more than that, that when he gazed at her with his oh-so-blue eyes, she became aware of herself as a woman, something she hadn't felt in a very long time.

''Well, well. Look who is back.''

Savannah tensed slightly at the sound of the familiar voice. She looked up to see Officer Jason Sheller. Jason was the one man she worked with whom she didn't like. He was too handsome, too slick, too confident, and something about him had always made her skin crawl. Part of her aversion to the man came from the fact that he had tried to put the moves on her mere weeks after Jimmy's death.

''What do you want, Jason?'' she asked.

''I see you're reading up on the Maxwell case. Anything new?''

''Apparently not since I've been gone. I'm thinking about reinterviewing Virginia Maxwell. There's something here we've got to be missing.''

''She's staying at the Redbud,'' he said. She looked at him in surprise and he shrugged. ''The local gossip update. She couldn't stand to stay in their house alone.'' One of his dark eyebrows quirked upward. ''And the other local gossip has it that you were seen there one evening with a handsome stranger. What's the deal, Savannah, local guys aren't good enough for you? Haven't you heard I have a big gun?''

"Go away, Jason," she said with disgust. "Don't you have a speeder to ticket or a doughnut to eat?"

"Ha, very funny," he said, but to her relief he ambled away from her desk.

She tried to focus once again on rereading the material in the Maxwell case file but realized she was too antsy to sit still. Instead she headed to the Redbud Bed and Breakfast to reinterview Virginia Maxwell.

The interview yielded nothing new except the reminder that she'd found Virginia's response to her husband's murder rather odd and nothing during this interview had changed her impression.

The pretty blond woman had cried at the appropriate times and had cursed the person responsible, but to Savannah none of it had rung quite true.

As she drove back to the station she chided herself. Not all grief manifested itself in the same way for every person. Jimmy had loved her waist-length hair, and two days after his death, in a state of profound grief, she'd stunned her family and friends by cutting it all off.

If Virginia Maxwell was dealing with her grief by shopping and getting manicures, then who was Savannah to judge her?

She'd been back at the station for over an hour when the phone on her desk rang. She snatched it up. "Officer Tallfeather."

"Savannah?"

She hadn't realized before how pretty her name was, but coming from Riley, it sounded lovely. A crazy kind of pleasure swept through her. "Hi, Riley."

"I'm glad you're back at work."

"Me, too. I needed to get away from myself, if that makes sense."

"It makes perfect sense," he replied. "The best thing you can do for yourself is to keep busy."

It was good to hear his voice, to talk to somebody who had been through it all, somebody who understood. "The reason I'm calling," he continued, "is that you mentioned last time we talked how frustrated your brother is that they aren't letting him into your parents' home."

"That's right." Clay's mood had gotten progressively worse with each passing day, and Savannah suspected he was spending too much time alone in his home and drinking.

"This is probably an absolutely crazy idea."

"What? What's a crazy idea?"

"I know it hasn't been established that what happened to your parents and what happened to mine are linked."

She released a sigh of frustration. "I spoke with Glen about your case just a little while ago, and he refused to even consider the possibility that they're linked. He said your case is closed and…" She hesitated a moment, unsure if she should continue with what else the chief had said.

"And what?" A deep sigh filled the line. "I suppose he mentioned the speculation that my mother ran off with the local handyman."

"Apparently Glen has access to some files you don't have and had looked up the case, and yes, that's exactly what he mentioned."

Again another deep sigh. "My parents had befriended a man named John Barker who was learning disabled. He had no family and did odd jobs for people in Sycamore Ridge. About once a week or so my parents would hire him to do some little job and invite him to stay for dinner. Sometimes in the mornings John would stop by the house and have a cup of coffee with my mother. It was all very innocent, but some people tried to turn it into something ugly."

"So, what happened to this John?"

"Two days before the incident, my mom told me that John had gotten a job with a family in Oklahoma City and was very excited about it. He'd come by to tell my parents goodbye."

"So, the handyman disappeared around the same time that your mother disappeared," Savannah said.

"Yes, but I'm telling you there's no way in hell my mother killed my father, then ran off with John. I've never been more certain of anything in my life. I'm as certain about it as you are about your own mother's innocence."

She believed him, and the more she'd thought about the two cases, the more she couldn't help but think that somehow, someway they had to be connected. "So, what does all of this have to do with Clay's frustration?" she asked.

"At the time of my father's murder, of course their house was gone over by the police, but once the crime-scene people were done with it, I locked it up and it's been locked up ever since. I just thought maybe Clay would like to get inside and see if the original officers overlooked something.''

Savannah's pulse rate increased at the thought. Was it possible Clay could find something in Riley's parents' home that might help them figure out what had happened to their parents? Something that might point to the whereabouts of their mother?

''You wouldn't mind us going inside?'' she asked.

''Not if it would help.''

She frowned thoughtfully. ''Why don't we tentatively plan to meet around four tomorrow afternoon and I'll talk to Clay about it tonight.''

''Sounds good to me.''

''And if for some reason that time won't work for Clay, I'll call you back.''

''Whatever works for the two of you will be fine with me. You've got the address. Do you need directions?''

''No, we should be able to find it without any problems.''

''Then I'll see you tomorrow at four.''

She told herself the excitement she felt was all about being able to reprocess a crime scene that might yield some information. She told herself it had nothing to do with the fact that she was going to see Riley again.

That evening, after getting off duty, she drove directly from the station to her brother's house. Clay lived on the outskirts of Cherokee Corners, in a small ranch house that was isolated from its neighbors by miles of dusty earth.

Silhouetted against the setting sun were several old, no-longer-working oil pumps. They resembled big-headed insects crouching in the dust.

Clay's car was out front so she knew he was home. She knocked on the front door, then pushed it open. "Clay?"

"In the kitchen," his deep voice replied.

She walked through the sterile living room, the room decorated with more lab equipment than actual furniture. She found her brother seated at the kitchen table, a handful of reports spread out before him.

"What are you looking at?" She sat across from him at the table.

"Preliminary lab reports of the forensic findings from Mom and Dad's." He didn't look up from the paper he held in his hand.

Savannah raised an eyebrow in surprise. "How did you get them?"

"Jesse brought them to me." Jesse Sampson was one of the three crime-scene investigators for the county.

"If Glen finds out you have those Jesse could get fired," she observed.

He looked up, his eyes the darkness of a cold, moonless night. "I don't intend to tell Glen…do you?"

"Of course not."

Clay threw the paper down on the table and took a long drink from a bottle of beer. "It doesn't matter anyway. So far the tests have yielded nothing to point to a suspect.''

"Have you eaten anything today?'' she asked, noting the empty beer bottles that peeked out of the nearly overflowing trash can.

"I'm not hungry.''

"You have to eat.'' She got up from the table and walked over to the refrigerator. She opened it up, unsurprised to see a variety of bottles of chemicals, solvents and items she didn't recognize but had nothing to do with foodstuff. She also spied a package of bologna and some slices of cheese.

"How about you eat a sandwich and I talk to you about something that might or might not interest you.''

"What are you talking about?''

She waited until he was eating before telling him about Riley and the crime that had happened two years before. Clay listened intently, his dark gaze giving away nothing of his inner thoughts.

Although he was her brother, she'd always found him an enigma, impossible to read, difficult to know. Oh, she knew he loved her and Breanna and their mother and father...at least as much as he was capable of loving.

"So, what do you think?'' she asked after she'd told him about the pending meeting with Riley the next day.

"I think it sounds like a waste of time,'' he said flatly. "I mean, what's the point? The scene was processed a long time ago.''

"But you're the best, Clay. If the original officers missed anything, you'll find it. You always find things nobody else does. What if the two cases are linked? What if you go to Riley's parents' house and do a little work and you find out what happened there? What happened to Mom and Dad?"

He reached across the table, grabbed her hand and squeezed. His eyes held the dark pain of a tortured soul. "We fought, you know. The last time I saw Mom, we had a terrible fight."

"About what?" Savannah asked.

"It doesn't matter what the fight was about…but I keep thinking, what if I never get a chance to apologize…to tell her that I love her." He released his hold on her hand, but she grabbed it once again.

"You will get a chance to apologize," she said fervently. "And you'll get a chance to tell her how much you love her. She's just missing, Clay. If it were anything else, we'd know. If she was really gone, surely we'd feel it in our hearts."

"You don't really believe that, do you?" This time he pulled his hand away and wrapped it around his beer bottle.

"I believe she's still alive." An ache pierced Savannah's heart as she thought of her mother. "I don't know. Maybe *we* wouldn't know if she was gone, but Alyssa would."

Clay finished his beer and tossed the bottle into the garbage. "Okay, I'll process the old crime scene and see if it yields any clues." His jaw clenched for a moment. "At least it will be better than sitting around here waiting for Dad to wake up, waiting for any news.''

''Good.'' Savannah stood, leaned over and kissed her brother on the forehead. ''Why don't I meet you here about three tomorrow afternoon. We can drive to Sycamore Ridge together.''

''All right,'' he agreed, and for the first time since that night of horror at her parents' home she saw life flicker in his eyes.

Tomorrow, she thought as she drove home minutes later. Tomorrow she'd see Riley, and perhaps tomorrow they'd get some answers.

Chapter 6

Riley sat in the driveway of his parents' home, dreading the moment when he would enter it again. A hundred times in the past two years he'd dreamed of going inside to find his mother and father seated at the card table in the living room, stewing over their latest, intricate jigsaw puzzle.

He knew that particular scenario would never happen, that his father was never coming back from the grave. But he did still hope that one day his mother would return from wherever she'd been with a logical explanation for her absence.

He hadn't been parked in the driveway for long when the car interior grew too hot. He got out and walked to the porch and sat on the stoop. Although he dreaded going into the house, he was looking forward to seeing her again.

Savannah. He wasn't sure why she'd lodged in his brain the way she had, from the moment he'd met her. Even now if he closed his eyes and focused he could smell the scent of her, visualize the rich darkness of her short hair, the beauty of that smile he'd seen in the photographs.

Over the past couple of days he'd tried to tell himself that what he felt was a crazy infatuation, that his life had been so isolated for so long that of course he would be attracted to a woman as pretty as Savannah.

But, no matter how he tried to convince himself that it was simply a passing infatuation, he couldn't. He'd never been the kind of man given to flights of fancy where women were concerned. It took far more than a pretty face or a killer body to pique his interest. And he couldn't make himself believe that his only interest in her was as a companion victim.

He saw the white panel van approaching and stood. He recognized that kind of van. One just like it had pulled in front of this house on the night of his father's murder. He just hadn't expected Clay and Savannah to arrive in such a vehicle. But it was them, and they pulled into the driveway and got out.

For a brief moment Riley drank in the sight of Savannah. The white shorts she wore not only showed off the length and shapeliness of her legs, but also complemented her cinnamon-bronze skin tones.

Her blouse was sleeveless and red, tied at her slender waist and opened at the neck to expose delicate collarbones. White strappy sandals adorned her feet, and her toenails were painted scarlet red.

He forced his attention away from her and to the man who accompanied her. It was the same man he'd suspected was her sibling the night he'd seen them together at her parents' home.

"Hi, I'm Riley Frazier," he said, and held out a hand.

"Clay. Clay James."

His handshake was strong and lasted only a moment. He nodded curtly, then rounded the back of the van and opened the doors.

"Clay isn't real good with people," Savannah said as if to apologize for her brother's brusqueness.

"He seemed fine to me," Riley replied. "How are you doing?"

She shrugged. "I'm as okay as I can be under the circumstances. We're still waiting for Dad to regain consciousness and hoping he can tell us what happened." She looked toward the house. "Are you sure you're okay with this?"

He glanced at the house and felt every muscle in his body tense at the prospect of going inside. He looked back at her and forced a smile. "I'm as okay as I can be under the circumstances."

She flashed him a smile that shored up his strength, made him believe he could face going back into the scene of his father's murder if it helped her in any way.

"Are we going to do this or what?" Clay peered around the back of the van at the two of them.

Savannah touched Riley's arm and gestured for him to follow her to the back of the van. Once there

Clay handed each of them gloves and plastic booties. "I don't know how much good this will do," he said. "But we might as well try not to contaminate anything that might be left inside."

Clay grabbed two steel suitcases, then the three of them walked to the front door. Riley was surprised to see his hand shake slightly as he reached out to unlock it. He hoped neither Savannah nor Clay had noticed.

He opened the door, noticing immediately that the air smelled musty…like a house that had been closed up for far too long. He was almost grateful for the foreign scent. The house no longer smelled like home.

Clay followed him in and set the two suitcases down on the foyer floor. As he bent down to open them, Savannah entered the house.

Riley drew a deep breath and stepped into the living room. Here the aftermath of murder still lingered. Fingerprint dust remained on the furniture, blood still stained the carpet around where his father's chair had been. The chair itself had been taken away by the police on the night of the murder.

Riley had believed his muscles were already taut, but now he felt them tighten even more. He needed to be strong. He wanted to be strong. He couldn't think about the last time he'd been in this room, when his father's body had been sprawled on the floor, the back of his head a bloody mass of tissue and brain matter.

He jumped as Savannah touched his arm. He turned

to look at her, hoping she didn't feel, couldn't see how close he was to shattering into a million pieces.

"It's the natural way of things that children bury their parents, but not like this," he said. "No child, no matter how old, should have to go through something like this."

"I know," she said softly. "Unfortunately, as a homicide detective I see this all too often."

He turned to look at her. "How do you get through the days?"

"I remind myself that I'm doing something good, that maybe with my work, a murderer will be taken off the streets and put behind bars for the rest of their lives."

"That's what I want to happen to the person who killed my dad. I'm not a vengeful man, but in this case I make an exception."

She nodded. "I know exactly how you feel."

"If you don't mind, Riley, I'd like to do a complete walk-through of the house before I really get down to business," Clay said.

Riley was grateful for the all-business tone in Clay's voice. For just a moment he'd felt himself getting far too emotional for comfort. "Fine with me. Why don't we start in the kitchen."

The walk-through was difficult. In every room there was evidence of lives suspended. In the kitchen a drainer held a rack of clean dishes, a dish towel covering them. His mother had rarely used the electric dishwasher, preferring to hand wash any dishes. She called the time it took her to hand wash dishes her think time.

In the bathroom a towel hung over the shower door and Riley remembered how much his mother had hated it when his father didn't put his towel in the hamper.

Both Clay and Savannah remained quiet as he led them through the house. He was grateful for their silence, felt as if it was somehow respectful of the people who had once lived here, loved here.

Savannah was the first to speak. They entered the bedroom where Riley had grown up, the room that his parents had kept much as it had been when he'd been a teenager. She walked over to the bookcase and looked at the trophies displayed there.

"A football jock, huh?"

"I played a little ball," he replied, oddly embarrassed by her peek into his past.

"Looks like you played pretty well—All-State Champion."

"We had a good team that year. I don't think there's anything in here that can help us."

"You're probably right," Clay agreed as if sensing his discomfort.

The master bedroom was the most difficult. Here was the evidence the initial investigators had thought proved that his mother had been responsible for his father's murder. Drawers were open, clothes spilling out as if items had been grabbed hurriedly. Several empty hangers dangled in the closet, some had fallen to the floor.

There was no denying that it appeared as if somebody had packed in a hurry. "Unless my mother tells me she's responsible for this, I'll never believe she packed up and ran away," he said. "Besides, even if the worst-case scenario is true, that somehow she suffered some kind of temporary insanity and hit my father, she never would have left without her treasure box."

"Treasure box?" Savannah looked at him curiously.

He went inside the closet and from the shelf above the clothes removed a wooden container the size of an old-fashioned breadbox. He placed it on the edge of the bed and opened it, aware of Clay and Savannah moving closer to see what the box contained.

Inside were a number of items—a baby photograph of Riley, the invitation to his parents' wedding, a dried corsage from a long-ago prom. There was also money. Lots of money. "Mom and Dad never took a honeymoon," Riley said. "So, Mom was saving up enough money for them to take one, last year on their anniversary. There's a little over a thousand dollars in here." He looked from Savannah to Clay. "Why would a woman on the run not take this money with her?"

Savannah and Clay exchanged a look. "You just made me remember something about our mother," Savannah explained. "She had a secret hiding place in her headboard. She kept her good jewelry there along with some cash."

"Was it taken?" Riley asked.

"I don't know. I don't think anyone ever checked."

"Let me know what you find out. I'd be interested to know," Riley replied.

From the master bedroom they returned to the living room and suddenly Riley needed to get out, get some air. He'd thought he'd be able to handle being inside the house again, but he couldn't. A sharp grief ripped through him with jagged edges that pierced his heart.

"You do whatever it is you need to do. I'll be out back on the patio," he said. He didn't wait for either of them to reply, but headed outside through the sliding glass doors in the living room.

The heat of the sun as he sat on one of the deck chairs warmed the chill that had taken possession of him. Two years—for almost two years his mother had been missing.

He leaned his head back and gulped the air that was filled with the sweet scent of roses. The scent came from a dozen rosebushes in the backyard, each one laden with blooming, rich-colored flowers.

How long before he got some answers? How long would he keep this house just as it was…waiting for the return of a woman who might never return?

He frowned at this thought. He couldn't think that way. She would come back. Somehow, someway, she'd return. He had to hold on to that thought.

There was nothing Savannah could do to help Clay. First and foremost she wasn't trained in his field, and secondly, her brother had always worked best when left alone.

She moved to the sliding doors and looked out to where Riley sat with his back to her in a plastic deck chair. She wasn't sure if he needed some time alone or would prefer company.

She'd seen his anguish with each step they'd taken through the house, had felt his anguish echoing inside of her. He'd given them a stiff upper lip, but his emotions had shown in the slight shake of his hands, his jaw muscles that clenched and unclenched and the pain that radiated from his blue eyes.

"I'm going outside. Call me if you need me to do anything," she said to her brother. He grunted in reply, his concentration completely focused on his task.

If Riley needs to be alone, then I'll know it and come back inside, she told herself as she slid the door open and stepped outside.

She sat in the deck chair right next to his but focused her attention on the lovely roses, giving him an opportunity to compose himself if he needed to. "The roses are gorgeous and smell wonderful," she said.

"My father planted them about six years ago after my mother complained he never brought her flowers. He said this way every spring and summer day she'd have flowers from him."

She looked at him then, saw that some of the grim lines that had etched into his face while they'd been inside the house had gone. "I'm sorry, Riley. I'm sorry you had to come here again."

He smiled, but it was a sad kind of smile. "It was my idea. You didn't force me into it."

"I know, but still…it has to be hard."

"I hadn't anticipated it being as hard as it was," he confessed. He drew a deep breath and sat up straighter in the chair. "But, it's nice out here. I've always liked this backyard."

"You like picnics?" she asked.

"Only if they include the food from the important food groups…thick sandwiches, potato salad and chocolate cake for dessert."

She laughed. "Ah, a fellow chocoholic."

"Definitely. I've been known to eat a handful of M&Ms and call it lunch, much to Lillian's disgust."

"Lillian?"

"Lillian is the feistiest sixty-two-year-old woman you ever want to meet. I hired her as a secretary six months ago, and she's become both a friend and a nagging surrogate mother figure."

"If she makes you eat more than M&Ms for lunch, then she's definitely worth her weight in gold," Savannah observed.

"And she reminds me of that every day," he replied.

His eyes had lightened, the darkness that had clung to them gone the longer they spoke of mundane things. "Tell me what else you like beside picnics," she said, wanting the pleasant conversation to continue.

He leaned back in the chair and stretched his long legs out before him, his gaze going to the rose bushes in the distance. "I like pepperoni pizza and a warm fire on a cold winter night. I like walking the land of Riley Estates and envisioning what will eventually be built there. I like getting up early enough to see a sunrise. Now, your turn."

For a moment her mind went blank. It had been so long since she'd thought about the things that brought her pleasure. "I like mushroom pizza," she began. "I like curling up with a good novel, working at the Cherokee Cultural Center and cats."

"Cats? I didn't see any cats when I was at your house."

"That's because I don't have one." She and Jimmy had talked about getting a cat many times, but had never gotten around to actually doing it. It was one of the promises they'd made for a future time…like anniversaries…and children…and love forever.

"Why not?" he asked.

"I don't know. I guess it's just one of those things you talk about but never actually take the time to do." In truth, after Jimmy's death she hadn't wanted to be responsible for any living thing.

"Life is pretty short," Riley said. "If you want a cat, you should get yourself one. They're pretty low maintenance from what I hear." He tilted his head and studied her for a long moment. "I would bet you're a low-maintenance kind of woman."

"What does that mean?" she asked, unsure if the observation should offend her or not.

"It's easier to explain if I tell you what a high-maintenance kind of woman is like. Take Patsy, for instance. She was definitely high maintenance. We couldn't go out if the wind was blowing and might mess up her hair. If it was too cold her lips got chapped, if it was too warm she felt faint. And I can't tell you how many meals got sent back to the kitchen when we ate out because they didn't meet her requirements.''

Savannah laughed. ''My hair is too short to get messed up in a tornado. I have chapped lips most of the time and I've never met a meal that I didn't like.''

Riley grinned. ''Definitely low maintenance and that's a nice thing.''

They continued to talk as dusk shadows deepened and Clay turned on lights in the house that radiated out to the back patio. The dark of night finally swallowed up the purple shadows of night and still Clay worked inside and still Riley and Savannah sat outside, talking and then falling into occasional comfortable silences.

The tension she'd felt radiating from him when she'd first come outside was gone and she sought to continue with a topic that would further relax him. ''What's your favorite season, Riley?''

''Any of them except winter. For a builder the enemy is always winter. What about you? What's your favorite?''

''I love the one we're in,'' she said without hesitation. ''Jimmy used to tell me that I was probably the only woman on earth who didn't complain about the cold in the winter, the heat in the summer and the wind in the spring and fall.''

"Jimmy...he was your husband." Curiosity lit his eyes. "Tell me about him."

It was odd, to have somebody ask about him. Since the time of his death nobody had wanted her to talk about Jimmy. Move on, they'd told her. Don't dwell on it. Now he wanted her to tell him about the man who had been her best friend, the man she had intended to spend the rest of her life with.

"I'm not sure where to begin," she said, fighting the grief that always accompanied thoughts of Jimmy.

"How did you meet him?"

"That's easy. When I was four, my mother and Jimmy's mother decided to do something to honor the Cherokee heritage. They were instrumental in getting the cultural center in Cherokee Corners started." As she spoke of distant days of childhood, some of the grief subsided. "Anyway, Jimmy was four years old, too. From the very beginning, we were great friends."

"That must have made his loss doubly hard," he said, his voice so soft, so gentle it brought a sudden burn of tears to her eyes as she nodded.

Jimmy. Dear Jimmy, her heart cried. "There are times it's still so hard. He was so much a part of my life. He was such a good man...a kind man."

"What did he do for a living?"

"He'd been a salesman, but he wasn't very good at it. He didn't like to push people, wasn't aggressive enough to be in sales. So, we'd agreed he should take some time and go back to school. He was driving home from night classes the night he crossed the old bridge and hit the guard rail."

Emptiness. She could still feel the emptiness she'd felt when the officers had arrived on her doorstep to give her the news. It had been a cold, hollow emptiness that, at times, still held her in its grip.

She'd thought of taking Riley's hand to offer support when she'd first come outside. But now it was he who reached for her hand, and she welcomed the warmth that seemed to flow straight to her heart.

"There are times you wonder how much suffering the human spirit can endure."

"I guess everyone's threshold for suffering is different. There are some nights I climb up in the girders of that old bridge and stare at the water beneath and wonder if I've finally reached my threshold of pain." The moment the words left her lips she was appalled that she'd confessed such a thing.

Before she knew what was happening, Riley stood and jerked her up before him. His fingers bit into the skin at her shoulders. "My God, Savannah. Surely you don't go up there and contemplate...even entertain for one moment the desire to...to..." He broke off, as if finding the thought too horrible to be spoken aloud.

He grabbed her to his chest, wrapped his arms around her and held her tight against him. She wanted to protest, but his arms were so strong, his chest so broad, and it had been so achingly long since she'd been held.

"If you ever, ever feel desperate and as if you can't go on, you call me. I'll help you get through the dark hours until you get strong again."

His words once again brought tears to her eyes. How long had it been since anyone had cared about those dark hours? Her family members had long ago quit talking about her loss, as if to stop speaking of it would make her heal more quickly.

His body was so warm against hers, and the warmth, coupled with the pleasure of their conversation, made her linger in his arms when she knew she should move away.

His scent, that bold masculine fragrance filled her senses at the same time her fingers itched to touch the rich darkness of hair at the nape of his neck.

She fought the impulse and started to step out of his arms. But when she raised her head to look at him, her breath caught in her chest and she couldn't move an inch. Desire. It radiated from his eyes, a rich desire that drew her into the blue depths.

She knew he was going to kiss her, knew she should step away, break the moment, stop it from happening. But before she could do any of those things his lips were on hers.

Hot and hungry, his mouth demanded…and got a response from her. She was helpless against the sensual assault as his tongue touched first the tip of her teeth, then slid beyond. It was wrong—desperately wrong—but it felt so right, so wonderfully right.

The kiss seemed to last both a single moment and an eternity. She wasn't even sure if he was the one to end it or she did. She only knew that one moment his mouth possessed hers, and the next moment it didn't.

She stumbled back from him with a surprised "Oh."

"Savannah."

"I've done everything I can here." Clay's voice boomed from the back door, interrupting whatever Riley had been about to say.

He stepped outside and looked at them expectantly. "Are we ready to take off? I've got some tests I'd like to get to right away."

Couldn't Clay feel the tension in the air…the thick, sexual tension that crackled and snapped between her and Riley? Savannah could certainly feel it. Not only could she feel the invisible tension, but her lips still felt hot and her heart pumped an irregular rhythm and she found it impossible to meet Riley's gaze.

"I'm ready when you are," she said to Clay. She forced herself to look at Riley. "Thank you for letting us in here."

His eyes held a dozen unspoken questions and the whisper of a still-simmering desire. "You'll let me know what you find?" he asked Clay.

"Of course," Clay replied.

"And, Savannah? I'll call you?"

She hesitated a moment, then nodded. "Okay."

For once in her life Savannah was grateful Clay wasn't a talker as they drove back to Cherokee Corners. She didn't want to talk. Over and over again she replayed those moments when his lips had been on hers, when his arms had held her tight. Over and over again her body flushed with heat as she remembered the bliss of his kiss.

It was nearly eleven by the time they got back to Clay's house and Savannah got into her car to drive home. She was nearly home when she realized it was Saturday night...her night to go to Jimmy.

Guilt ripped through her as she realized she'd nearly forgotten. The blackness of despair crept over her, through her. How could she have allowed one simple little kiss to make her forget Jimmy?

Riley had told her to call him when she felt like going to the bridge, but he didn't understand... couldn't understand the despair that drove her there. Nobody could understand.

Tonight her despair was worse than ever as she thought of how easily she'd fallen into the sensual play of Riley's lips on hers. She felt as if she'd betrayed Jimmy, her husband, the love of her life.

Before she knew it, she was at the old bridge, and it took her only minutes to climb the familiar path amid the girders over the dark water of the Cherokee River.

Shame washed over her, not the shame of kissing another man, but the shame of enjoying the kiss of another man. She had promised to love Jimmy through eternity, had vowed that he would always be the only man in her heart.

"You're my woman, Savannah." Jimmy's deep voice echoed in her head. "We were destined to be together...forever...for always."

For just a moment she'd allowed herself to indulge in the possibility of another relationship, another man. Jimmy deserved better than that.

"I'm sorry, Jimmy," she whispered, looking to the water beneath her.

She was overwhelmed, guilt ridden by the fact that she'd enjoyed Riley's company, enjoyed his kiss. She was twisted into knots by the trauma and uncertainty of her parents' well-being. Things had become just so hard. Life had become so difficult.

Her mother was gone, her father in a state of limbo and she was lonely...so very lonely. Why hang on? Why face another day? What was the point of getting up in the morning? Going on with her empty life?

"Jimmy." She tried to feel the same anguish she'd felt the last time she'd been here, the strong desire to jump and join him in the spirit world. She closed her eyes against the tears that burned.

If she did jump she would be in the arms of her husband forever. She wouldn't have to deal with the unanswered questions where her father and mother were concerned. She could just let go...let go of life and be released from all pain.

But when she looked down at the river, it was Riley's face she saw reflected on the water. His blue eyes shone like stars in her mind, his smile like the sun lighting up the sky. She squeezed her eyes tightly closed again, not wanting to think about him.

Jimmy...that's who she should be thinking about. Jimmy, who had loved her so deeply, who had been her soul mate. Jimmy deserved her love, her devotion.

The ringing of her cell phone shattered the silence of the night and her thoughts. She ignored the first four rings, but whoever was trying to get in touch with her was persistent, for the phone kept on ringing.

She finally answered.

"Savannah?" A subdued excitement filled the voice of her sister, Breanna. "You've got to get over here to the hospital. Daddy's waking up."

Chapter 7

By the time Savannah arrived at the hospital, Scott Moberly was skulking around in the lobby. "Hey, Savannah." His boyish features lit up as he spied her coming through the double door. "I heard your father's waking up."

"That's what I've heard, too." Savannah didn't stop her progress toward the door that led to the patient rooms.

"Will you tell me what he says…"

Scott's voice disappeared as the door closed behind her. Ahead of her, down the distance of the long hallway, she saw a group of people gathered outside her father's door. Breanna and Adam were there, as well as Clay and Glen Cleberg.

Breanna and Adam saw her first and hurried to meet her. "Dr. Watkins is in there with Dad now."

"How's he doing? Can he speak? Has he said what happened to him? To Mom?" The bridge she'd just climbed down from seemed very far away as adrenaline pumped through her.

"We don't know anything yet," Adam said. "The doctor has been in there with him since we all arrived."

The three of them joined the others who stood just outside the closed door.

"Who called Moberly?" Savannah asked. "He was perched like a vulture in the lobby when I came in.

"The little twerp was hanging around at the station when the call came in about your dad," Glen explained. "I'd put the word in that I wanted to be notified immediately if there was any change in Thomas's condition."

Before anyone could say anything else, Dr. Watkins stepped out of the room and into the hallway. They all converged on him, and he held up his hands to silence them.

"He's awake and he's talking. But it appears he's suffered some damage to his motor control. He's confused and a bit disoriented, so we're going to make your visits brief. You can go in a couple at a time for a few minutes."

It was decided that Breanna, Adam and Clay would go in first. "I do not want him upset," Dr. Watkins said. "I know you're all eager to get some answers, but I don't want him pushed. He's quite fragile right now, and I won't have him set back by everyone demanding more than he can give at the moment."

He followed the first group into the room while Savannah and Glen remained in the hallway.

"When are you going to let Clay come back to work?" she asked her boss.

"I thought maybe he already returned to work without my notice. The CSI van was missing for several hours this evening." He cocked an eyebrow. "Want to tell me what that was all about?"

Instantly her head filled with the memory of Riley's kiss, that heavenly, hot kiss that had given her a moment of pleasure and more time of torment.

"Savannah?"

Even though she knew he'd be irritated, she told Glen about going to Sycamore Ridge and Clay reprocessing the old Frazier crime scene.

"That case is closed," Glen exclaimed. "Your afternoon there was a waste of time."

"Maybe," she agreed. "But keeping Clay out of his lab and away from his work is a waste of his talent."

"You James people hang tighter than anyone I know," Glen said irritably. "I've already heard it all from your sister when she got here."

"Clay needs to work. That's all he has at the moment to keep him sane."

"I'm releasing the house tomorrow," Glen said. "We've done all we can there. And if I know Clay, the minute I tell him the house is released he'll be over there reprocessing that scene." Glen shoved his hands in his pockets and leaned again the wall. "Who knows, maybe he'll be able to pick up something we missed."

Before they could speak further, Breanna, Adam and Clay filed out of the room. Breanna was teary-eyed but smiling, and Adam leaned over and whispered something in her ear and her smile grew brighter as love for him poured from her gaze.

A thick shaft of envy struck at Savannah's heart. How lucky Bree was to have someone to hold her hand, support her and love her.

She thought of Riley's hand...so big...so warm and with just enough rough edges to be interesting. She frowned. Why was she thinking of Riley's hand? She should be remembering the feel of Jimmy's hand holding hers.

Dr. Watkins appeared at the door and motioned to Savannah and Glen. Savannah went in first and her heart swelled to fill her chest at the sight of her father's familiar blue eyes gazing at her.

"Daddy," she said, and rushed to his side as Glen remained standing just inside the doorway.

"Savannah...my shining Silver Star." Although the words were slurred, they were intelligible, and a vast relief swept through her. He was lucid enough to know who she was, to remember her Cherokee name, and he could talk. At the moment nothing else seemed quite as important.

She took his right hand, which remained limp and unresponsive in hers. "You've had us all so very worried."

"Sorry." His eyes held bewilderment. "Where's your mama...why isn't she here with me?"

Savannah exchanged a look with Glen, who stepped up to the foot of Thomas's bed. "Do you know how you got hurt, Thomas?" Glen asked.

Thomas frowned and with his left hand reached up and touched the swath of bandages on the back of his head. "Did I fall?"

"Don't you remember?"

Panic filled Thomas's eyes. "Am I supposed to remember?" His frantic gaze went from Glen, to Savannah, then back to Glen. "Where's Rita? She'll remember. I don't...I can't..."

"Shh, it's all right, Dad," Savannah assured him, and shot a warning look to Glen. "You just rest now. You rest and get better, stronger. That's what's important."

Thomas closed his eyes as the doctor motioned them out of the room. Dr. Watkins led them some distance down the hallway, then turned to face them all.

"I know you're all anxious for answers. But I have to warn you that there's a possibility you won't ever get any from Thomas. It isn't unusual for victims of severe trauma to have no memory of the incident that lands them in a hospital."

An intense disappointment swept through Savannah, and she knew it was the same emotion every one of them were feeling. They had so hoped that when Thomas came awake answers would quickly follow.

"That's it for tonight," Dr. Watkins continued. "I

want my patient to rest. And there will be no visitors allowed tomorrow. We'll be running a full battery of tests to determine the full extent of damage and working up a rehabilitation program. You all can visit him again tomorrow evening.''

Minutes later the James siblings all sat in the empty hospital cafeteria. They were seated at one of the round tables, each with a cup of stale coffee in front of them.

''Okay, so we know now that it's possible Dad won't be able to tell us anything about that night,'' Breanna said. ''I think it's time we get more proactive about doing something to find Mom.''

''What do you suggest, Bree? We've done everything we can think of,'' Savannah replied.

''Adam and I were talking last night and we think it might be a good idea to get some posters printed up and distributed around the county.''

''Glen already had her picture flashed on the evening news,'' Clay said.

''But that was just for two nights, and the picture was only shown briefly. We need posters to keep Mom's face in front of people,'' Bree explained.

''I'll see to the printing if you will help with the distribution,'' Adam said.

Clay shrugged. ''I guess it can't hurt.'' Savannah nodded her agreement.

''Has anyone checked in at the cultural center?'' Savannah asked. This was the busiest season at the tourist attraction and she wondered how they were getting along without her mother's drive, enthusiasm and organizational skills.

"I spoke with Mary yesterday. Everything is hectic, and they miss Mom desperately, but they're functioning as best they can. I'm planning on helping out whenever possible. It would be nice if you two would step up to the plate and give them some time, as well," Bree said.

"I'll call Mary tomorrow," Savannah said. Clay said nothing and both sisters knew he wouldn't be offering any of his time or services there.

Clay refusing to have any part of the cultural center had been a continuous source of friction between him and his mother, and Savannah wondered if perhaps that had been what they'd fought about before her disappearance.

In any case it didn't matter. Savannah made a mental note to herself to call and see if there was anything she could do to help with the work that was dearest to her mother's heart.

It was agreed that they would meet the following night at Breanna and Adam's house to pick up posters for distribution.

Exhaustion weighed heavily on Savannah as she drove home from the hospital.

It had been more than a full day. First she'd wrestled with the Maxwell case for several hours at the station, trying to glean any clues that might have been missed, clues that might lead to a murderer. Then the emotional trauma of joining Riley in his parents' house...a house of death that still held the vestiges of a son's hopes.

If that hadn't been enough, there had been that kiss followed by her journey to the bridge and then the phone call that her father had come out of his coma.

The day had been a roller coaster of ups and downs, ins and outs that had left her physically and emotionally depleted.

And still they knew nothing about what had happened to their mother.

Sleep came quickly to her that night, but it was a sleep filled with dreams. She dreamed of the river, and in her dream she clung to the bridge support over water that foamed and splashed with a restless energy.

Jimmy was there beneath the surface, his brown eyes pleading, his arms stretched out to her. She knew if she went to him, the worries of the world would no longer be carried in her heart. She was just about to let go, to join him in his watery grave when Riley appeared on the ground beneath her.

"Come to me, Savannah," he said, his piercing blue eyes holding the promise of new passion, of possibility. "Forget him."

"Silver Star, you are my woman forever and always." Jimmy's gaze held the bittersweet memories of childhood friendship, adolescent sexual awakening and adult love and commitment. "Forever and always."

She awoke with the perspiration of conflict dampening her body. She turned on her bedside lamp and swung her legs over the edge of the bed, trying desperately to shove away the remnants of the dream.

One thing was certain. Riley Frazier and that kiss they had shared was messing with her mind, making her think about things she shouldn't, dream about choices that shouldn't exist.

She didn't intend to see Riley Frazier again.

"That looks like a love-struck man if ever I've seen one." Lillian's voice pulled Riley back to the here and now.

He felt the heat of a blush work up his neck and wondered how long she'd been standing in his office doorway watching him stare out the window. "I just have a lot on my mind."

"A woman. Tell me the truth, you have a woman on your mind." She smiled knowingly. "I've seen men with that expression on their faces many times before, and it's always a woman that's in his head."

"Her name is Savannah Tallfeather," he said. And three days ago I kissed her, and that kiss was the best thing that's happened to me in two years. "She's a homicide detective over in Cherokee Corners."

One of Lillian's brows raised. "A homicide cop? Is she working on your father's case?"

"Yes and no." Briefly Riley explained to her the criminal connection between him and Savannah. "I went to her because I thought maybe the person responsible for her parents' crime was also responsible for mine."

"And what have you found out?"

Riley frowned. "Nothing conclusive. The situations are the same and her mother is missing like mine, but nothing specific to tie the two scenes together."

"And so your interest in Savannah Tallfeather is strictly professional, so to speak?" There was a distinct twinkle in Lillian's eyes.

"It might be a little more than that," Riley admitted after a moment of hesitation.

"Good," Lillian exclaimed decisively. "It's about time you got a woman in your life, time you moved away from your pain and loss and looked to the future."

"I do look to the future," Riley protested. He gestured out the window. "That's what Riley Estates is all about."

"That's your work future, that has nothing to do with your personal happiness. A man isn't all that he can be when he's alone, Riley. A man needs a woman, children to fulfill his complete potential."

Riley laughed. "For heaven's sake, Lillian, I barely know the woman."

Lillian studied him for a long moment. "Maybe so, but I haven't seen that particular spark in your eye since I've known you. Just saying her name makes your eyes light up, and if you have any sense at all, you'll pursue her with the same single-mindedness you've spent in your work."

Minutes later, with Lillian gone from the doorway, Riley once again focused his gaze out the window. In the distance he could see the dust rising in the air from the bulldozer clearing land for a new home site, but his thoughts were on Savannah.

In the three days since they had parted at his parents' home, he'd called her several times and left messages on her machine at work. She had not returned any of his calls.

The kiss had been a mistake. It had been entirely inappropriate and he half wished he could take it back. But the other half of him reveled in the memory of the sweet heat of her lips, her slender curves that had momentarily melded into him, the race of her heartbeat against his own.

He'd had no intention of kissing her when he'd pulled her into his arms, had known only a gut-wrenching fear for her when she'd confessed about her sojourns to the bridge.

She'd scared him half to death with her confession and he'd done the only thing he knew to do—pull her against him and hold her tight. If she hadn't looked up at him with her doe-soft eyes, he might have released her without the kiss. But the minute she'd looked at him, he'd been lost. And damn it, it had been too much, too soon.

He'd obviously scared her. He wanted to talk to her, to tell her that he was sorry if he'd overstepped the boundaries between them. But it was difficult to apologize when he couldn't get hold of her.

He hated to think that she was avoiding his phone calls, preferred to think that she'd simply been too busy to contact him. He'd heard from Scott that her father had come out of his coma but had been unable to remember anything about the night he'd been attacked.

Savannah Tallfeather certainly had many more important things on her mind than him and the kiss they had shared.

He stood and stretched, then looked at his wristwatch. It was almost five. Within ten minutes the crew would be knocking off for the day and he felt like a drive.

"I'm out of here," he said to Lillian as he left his office. "I'll have my cell phone with me if anything should come up in the next ten or fifteen minutes."

"I'm sure we'll be fine, boss," she assured him. "Enjoy your evening."

"You do the same, Lillian."

He thought he was going home, but was somehow unsurprised to find himself on the highway that would take him to Cherokee Corners.

He just wanted to talk to her, wanted to apologize, if an apology was necessary. He didn't want to do anything that would make her uncomfortable. He just wanted her to know that he was available to be a support to her in whatever way she might need him to be. No expectations. No strings attached.

The hour-long drive was nice. Riley felt himself unwinding from the day, putting the cares of the business behind him as he anticipated seeing Savannah again.

An officer had answered her work phone the day before and told him that Officer Tallfeather wasn't available at the moment but was working until five that evening.

It would be after six by the time he reached Cherokee Corners, and he was hoping he would find her at her apartment. If he didn't find her there, then he would drop in at the Redbud Bed and Breakfast and see if her cousin knew where she might be found.

He thought of what Lillian had said…about a woman and children making a man realize his full potential. He'd thought about children once upon a time, but the problem had been no matter how hard he tried, he couldn't imagine Patsy as a mother. The first time a baby spit up on her, or grabbed one of her perfectly coiled curls, she would have had a fit.

No, Patsy hadn't been mother material, but that didn't mean he wasn't father material. Someday, with the right woman, he'd love to have children, fill that big house of his with laughter and love. That had been his parents' dream for him, a dream he had forgotten about until now.

It was just after six when he pulled down Main Street of Cherokee Corners. On a whim he parked his truck in front of the Pet Palace. He thought of the conversation he and Savannah had shared and the desire she'd once had to own a cat.

I'll just take a look at what they have, he told himself as he entered the store. It would be highly presumptuous of him to actually get her a cat.

A cacophony of sound greeted him. Birds screeched, dogs barked and little furry critters scurried around in their cages as if seeking to capture his attention and find themselves a home.

He bypassed the hamsters, the fish and the squawking birds. He paused briefly in front of the dog cages, momentarily captivated by a white and black puppy of indeterminable parentage who shoved his food dish toward the front of the cage, then eyed Riley expectantly.

"We've nicknamed him Munch," a female voice said from behind Riley. He turned to see an older woman with a pleasant smile. "All he wants to do is eat."

Riley smiled. "He's cute, but I was actually interested in a cat."

"Ah, we have two lovely Persians that just came in."

Riley frowned. He had a feeling Savannah Tallfeather wasn't a Persian cat kind of woman. "I was thinking more like a tabby." Patsy was a Persian cat kind of woman, Savannah was definitely a tabby.

The saleslady led him to a large cage where half a dozen kittens were playing. As he moved closer they meowed loudly, as if vying for his attention, their little paws reaching out between the cage bars.

Again Riley wondered if this was a good thing to do or if it might just be a mistake, like the kiss might have been. Then he spied the kitten that sat on a perch at the back of the cage. So tiny—he knew it would fit in the palm of his hand—the yellow-striped tabby watched him silently.

"The one in the back...is it sick or something?"
He pointed to the little one.

"No, she's just one of the most laid-back kittens
I've ever seen."

Exactly what Savannah needed, he thought. If he
bought her a cat, maybe it would keep her off that
bridge. Maybe she needed something alive and solely
dependent on her.

And if it was a mistake and she didn't want the
kitty, then he'd keep her. Twenty minutes later he left
the pet store with not only the kitten but everything
a cat might need to live a comfortable life—food, toys
and a super scooper litter box.

He drove from the pet store to Savannah's apartment complex, pleased to see her car parked in the
space in front of her apartment.

With the kitten in the crook of his arm, he walked
up to her door, surprised to find himself more nervous
than he could remember being in a very long time.

She opened the door, and any nervousness he'd
momentarily suffered instantly left him. She looked
beautiful, clad in a rose-colored robe and with her hair
tousled as if she'd just awakened from a nap.

"Riley!" It was obvious by the expression on her
face that he was the last person she had expected to
see.

"Can we come in?" he asked.

"We?" Her gaze shot beyond his shoulder, as if
anticipating another person standing nearby.

"We." He held out the kitten.

"Oh, Riley, what have you done?" She opened the

door to let him in, and he walked ahead of her to the living room and sat down on the sofa.

"Look, if you aren't interested in taking her in, it's not a problem," he said hurriedly. "I just remembered you mentioning the other day that you'd always wanted a cat."

She sat down next to him, so close he could smell the familiar scent of her, that feminine flowery fragrance that made his pulse beat just a little bit faster.

She leaned over and took the kitten from him, and as she did, her robe gaped open slightly, exposing delicate collarbones and something silky and pink beneath the robe. "Where'd you find her?" she asked.

"The Pet Palace."

The kitten curled up in her lap and as she stroked the soft reddish-blond fur, a noisy purr filled the silence. She looked tired, Riley thought as she gazed down at the cat. She wore no makeup, and purple shadows dusted the skin just beneath her eyes.

He felt like an adolescent, wondering if he should apologize for the kiss, yet dreading the idea of bringing up the subject.

"I bought everything you'd need if you decide to keep her," he said, unable to stand the silence any longer. "All she needs is a name."

Savannah looked up at him, her gaze radiating bewilderment. "Why did you do this, Riley? What do you want from me?"

What did he want from her? He wasn't sure. He wanted to spend time with her. He wanted to kiss her again, but he couldn't very well tell her that. His gaze fell on one of the pictures of her and her husband.

"What do I want from you?" He pointed to the photograph. "I want to see you smile like that…like you have the world by the tail, like you have nothing but happiness ahead of you."

She stared at the picture for a long moment, and when she looked back at him her eyes were dark, almost haunted. "I don't think that's ever going to happen again," she said softly. "Riley, I…"

He heard the protest begin in her words, and he quickly jumped in to interrupt her. "To be honest, Savannah, the last couple of years have been difficult for me. I've kept myself too isolated from people, and I like you. I could use a friend, and I think you could use one, too. No strings attached, no expectations…just friendship."

He hoped as she studied his face she couldn't see how desperately he'd like to kiss her right now, right at this very moment. "Okay," she said, her voice still soft. "I'd like to be your friend—no strings attached, no expectations."

"And my gift?" He gestured to the kitten still curled up in her lap.

She smiled. "Is accepted with many thanks."

"Good." Riley stood. "I'll just go get the food and toys and things from my car." Friendship, it was a start, and he had a feeling it was all she was willing to give for now.

And he hadn't been lying. He wanted to see that smile she'd had in the photograph with her husband.

But he wanted to see that same kind of joyous, loving smile directed at him.

Yes, a friendship was a start, but he knew he would never be satisfied with just that from her.

Chapter 8

She'd made a conscious decision not to return his phone calls over the past three days. She told herself they really had nothing to say to each other. Clay was still processing the evidence he'd gathered at the Frazier house and none of Riley's messages indicated any urgency.

Even though she hadn't returned any of his calls, she had to confess to herself that seeing him standing at her door had sent a wave of pleasure through her.

As he went out to get the things he'd purchased for the kitten, she belted her robe more tightly around her, then carried the cat into the kitchen and set her on the floor so she could make a pot of coffee.

She couldn't believe he'd bought her a kitten, and such a sweet little baby at that. She couldn't believe he'd paid that much attention to the conversation they'd had on the back deck at his parents' home. For the past year she hadn't felt as if anyone listened when she spoke.

Friends. He'd said he'd like to be friends, no strings attached. There was no fooling herself about the fact that she could use a friend. She hadn't realized until after Jimmy's death that most of their friends had been his, and they had vanished soon after Jimmy.

For Savannah, her family had always been enough, but now her family was fragmented and there were moments when her feelings of isolation threatened to consume her.

But a friendship with Riley? Was that possible? They'd already overstepped the boundaries of friendship with the kiss they had shared, a kiss she'd had difficulty forgetting.

Once the coffeepot was steaming and spewing hot brew into the glass container, she picked up the kitten. At the same time Riley came back inside, his arms laden with supplies.

"My goodness, it looks like you bought out the place," she exclaimed.

"I bought the things I thought a kitten would need to live a long, healthy life."

"Obviously a long, healthy, pampered life," she said with a small smile as he unloaded the items on the floor near the kitchen table. "Let me repay you what you spent, Riley."

He looked shocked at the very notion. "A gift isn't a gift if the recipient pays for it. And she and everything that comes with her is a gift."

"Then, thank you." She looked down at the kitten, her heart filled as it hadn't been in a very long time.

"Now all you need to do is name her."

"Happy," she said without conscious thought, for that was what she felt at the moment.

"Sounds good to me," he agreed. "And that coffee smells great."

Minutes later, with Happy contentedly eating gourmet cat food, Savannah and Riley sat down at her kitchen table, each with a cup of coffee.

"Now, how are you? You look tired," he said.

"I am," she admitted. "The last couple of days have been frantic. I've been dividing my time between the hospital, work and distributing posters of my mom all around town. I came home from work tonight ready to collapse. I promised myself a night of doing nothing, so I took a long, hot bath and climbed into my nightgown and robe." Self-consciously she tugged on her belt once again.

"Then I'm interfering with your quiet time. I should go." He started to rise from his chair.

"No, it's fine," she said hurriedly. "Besides, now you have to stay and help me finish that pot of coffee."

He sank back down. "I heard your father came out of his coma."

"Yes, and he's recovering nicely. Unfortunately, he doesn't remember anything about the night he got hurt, and he needs some rehabilitation for some resulting weakness on the right side of his body."

"Has anyone told him yet about your mother being missing?"

"We had to tell him yesterday." Her heart ached as she remembered the tears her father had shed at the news. In all her thirty years she'd never seen her father weep until yesterday.

His tears had quickly transformed to bellows of rage when they told him the authorities thought Rita was responsible for his injuries. He'd called them stupid fools, shouted that it was impossible that his Rita had been responsible. It had been a heartrending scene.

"He believes, like all of us, that there's no way Mom could have done this to him then run away."

Riley shifted positions in his chair and the displacement of air around him sent a whisper of his scent wafting to her. He wore the smell of the outdoors, the fragrance of a sunshine-drenched shirt and an underlying hint of woodsy cologne.

It was a scent that provoked memories of what it had felt like to be held tight against his broad chest, feel the beat of his heart against her own.

"My uncle Sammy arrived in town yesterday," she said, trying to keep her mind focused on her life and not the man seated next to her. "He's my father's younger brother. He's going to be staying at the ranch now that the police have released it."

"Is that a good thing?" Riley asked.

"It will be good to have somebody there. None of us wanted to leave the place empty until Dad can go home. I probably would have been the one to stay out there, and to tell the truth, I wasn't sure I was ready for that.''

He nodded and she had the satisfaction of knowing he knew exactly what she was talking about. ''Are you and your uncle close?''

She smiled at thoughts of her uncle Sammy. ''Throughout our childhood Uncle Sammy was like this bigger-than-life hero who would swoop into our lives and turn everything topsy-turvy for a couple of days, and then disappear again. He was handsome and fun and always brought presents.'' She paused to take a sip of her coffee, then continued. ''Now that I'm older I see him a little differently.''

''How so?''

She startled as Happy jumped up in her lap. She scratched the kitten's head and frowned thoughtfully. ''Uncle Sammy is still handsome as the devil and can be a lot of fun. But I've come to realize he's also an irresponsible dreamer who has always chosen the easy way out of everything. He drifts from place to place looking for the next get-rich-quick scheme. He's had some brushes with the law, he's never worked a regular job and never has a permanent address.''

''So, he's kind of the black sheep of the family,'' Riley observed.

''More gray than black,'' she replied. ''What about you? Any black sheep in your family?''

''No family,'' he replied. ''My parents were only children, and I was an only child. I guess that's why I was so close to them…because it was always just the three of us.''

She doubted he even heard the depth of pain in his words, but she heard it and found it impossible not to be moved. She wanted to reach out and touch him, to stroke the back of his hand or place her fingers on the warm skin of his forearm, but she was afraid…afraid that if she touched him once, she'd want to touch him again…and again.

"Beside everything else that's going on, I'm in the middle of a murder investigation that's driving me insane," she said to change the subject.

"Want to talk about it?"

She shrugged. "Unfortunately, there isn't much to talk about. Greg Maxwell was found naked and stabbed in front of the public library on Main Street and we have no idea who's responsible."

"Oh yeah, I remember reading something about that when it happened." He stood and walked over to the coffeepot and refilled his cup, then hers. As he took the pot back to where it belonged, she couldn't help but notice how his jeans seemed to fit as if denim had been invented just for him.

She quickly shifted her attention back to the kitten in her lap, who was purring like the engine of a motorboat. He rejoined her at the table, his gaze curious. "So, no forensic clues in the case?"

"No, the scene was fairly well contaminated by the time Clay got there to collect evidence."

"What about motive? Who stood to gain something if Greg Maxwell was dead?"

Savannah raised an eyebrow. "You sound like a cop."

He grinned, the gesture lighting his eyes to an azure blue that nearly stole her breath away. "I watch a lot of television. So, any motive?"

"A fairly substantial life insurance policy for his wife."

"Ah, so there's your answer," he said. "Don't they say most homicides are committed by spouses?"

"That's the mentality that has our mothers as prime suspects," she said wryly.

"Touché." He frowned thoughtfully. "But statistically isn't it more likely than not in a homicide that the first suspect is always the spouse? And the other thing I've always heard is that cops follow the money, and that often leads to the guilty."

"Sure, and in the Maxwell case I haven't written off Virginia Maxwell as a suspect." It felt good to talk about the case with somebody who had a fresh eye, somebody she trusted completely. "There's something about her that doesn't quite ring true to me."

"What do you mean?"

Savannah stared down into her coffee cup, trying to discern just what it was about Virginia that didn't sit right with her. She looked back up at Riley, as always finding his direct blue gaze almost hypnotic.

"I don't know, maybe it's because I'm a widow, too. Her grief just doesn't feel deep enough, true enough. She says all the right things, but I just don't believe her."

"Does she have an alibi for the night of her husband's murder?" Riley asked.

Dead Certain

"According to her, Greg had spent the evening at the library and she'd had dinner with friends. After dinner she went home and fell asleep while waiting for Greg to return home. As an alibi, it's impossible to corroborate."

"But it's also difficult to think about a woman being able to strip a man naked and stab him to death," Riley said. "Especially if that man is her husband."

"That's what Glen thinks, too," she admitted. "But, women do kill…and sometimes they kill viciously. Whomever killed Greg knew him personally, of that I'm convinced."

"What makes you so sure?"

"He was stabbed in a frenzy and that indicates rage…a personal rage. Also, the fact that he was left naked suggests the perpetrator wanted him humiliated. I'm betting on Virginia having something to do with it and I'm checking into her background. And I've bored you long enough with all this talk about my work."

He smiled. "I don't find it boring at all. I find it fascinating, but you're right, that's enough shop talk. And I've taken up enough of your evening."

This time when he rose from the table she didn't attempt to stop him. All the talk about the Maxwell case had exhausted her and had reminded her of all the unanswered questions in the cases that were dearest to both her heart and Riley's.

She stood also, gently placing Happy on the floor, where the kitten stretched, curled up in a ball and went back to sleep. She walked with Riley to the door. "I can't thank you enough for Happy," she said.

"Yes, you can," he said, and turned to face her as they reached the front door. "The way you can thank me is by making me a promise."

"A promise?" She looked at him curiously.

He reached out a hand as if to touch her, but to her relief quickly dropped it back to his side. "You can promise me you'll stay off that bridge."

A hundred different emotions attacked her from all sides at his request. Anger that he would even presume to ask for such a promise, a tiny thrill that he would care, and the frustration that he obviously didn't understand, couldn't understand the constant grief that drove her.

"I can't do that, Riley, and you really have no right to ask that of me." She focused her gaze away from him, unable to look at him without fearing she might capitulate and make the promise to him. And she wasn't ready for that.

"You're right," he said with a deep sigh. "I apologize. I was just hoping as a friend who cares about you, I'd have the right to ask you that. Anyway...good night, Savannah." He leaned forward and gently pressed his lips to her forehead. "Sweet dreams."

For a long time after he'd left, Savannah felt the sweet burn of his lips on her forehead and a curious ache she couldn't identify in her heart.

She'd just settled down in bed with Happy curled contentedly at her feet when her cell phone rang. She struggled to sit up and reach for the offending instrument on her nightstand.

"Officer Tallfeather," she said.

"Savannah…it's Glen. We've got another one."

"Another one?"

"Sam McClane was found a little while ago behind the post office. He's naked and has been stabbed."

"I'm on my way."

Although she was exhausted, adrenaline shoved her out of bed and she was dressed and out the door within minutes. Although she dreaded what lay ahead, she was relieved for any distraction that would take her mind off Riley.

By the time she arrived at the scene, the county medical examiner was already there and the immediate area had been cordoned off. Clay was there, as well, gathering evidence that would hopefully give them some clues.

"Hey, Walter, what have you got for me?"

The elderly M.E. drew off his plastic gloves and shook his head. "I'd put time of death within the last two hours. Cause of death is multiple stab wounds to the chest. At first investigation it looks just like the Maxwell scene."

At that moment Glen Cleberg joined them, his brow deeply wrinkled with worry. "Who found him?" Savannah asked.

Glen jerked a thumb in the direction of the back of the post office building where a young man stood talking to one of the officers. "Name is Burt Sheffle. He works part-time cleaning some of the offices down here. He had just finished up inside the post office and was taking trash out to the Dumpster.''

"He look likely?" she asked.

"Not hardly. The kid's been puking his guts up since he found the body."

Savannah sighed. "I guess this shoots to hell my gut instinct that Virginia Maxwell killed Greg."

"Unless this is a copycat deal," Walter said.

"Let's hope it is," Glen replied. "Let's hope to hell it's a copycat."

Savannah knew what he was thinking. If it was a copycat, then that meant they had two murderers to find. If it wasn't a copycat, then it could be the beginning of something much more sinister. It could mean they had a brutal serial killer in the small town of Cherokee Corners.

The officers worked the scene until the first tentative colors of dawn spread across the sky. Only then did they finally take a break for coffee.

Savannah took her foam cup and carried it over to where her brother sat on the curb. She sank down next to him and took a sip of the hot, strong coffee.

"Hell of a business we're in," he said. "I spent all day processing our parents' house, and tonight I'm processing a new crime scene. I haven't been this busy since I started on the job."

"Did you find anything interesting at Mom and Dad's?" she asked.

"Fibers…hairs…the usual bag of tricks. I still need to separate, examine and categorize everything. I didn't find anything that looked like a sure-fire address to the perp.''

She smiled ruefully. "It never is that easy."

He sighed. "No, it isn't."

"You think we have a serial working?"

"I hope not...but this scene and Maxwell's are exactly the same. Fortunately there is less contamination at this one, so maybe something will turn up to help us find whoever did this."

"Let's hope so." She finished her coffee, then got back to work. The last of the sunrise streaked the sky when she finally headed home.

A serial killer. Was it really possible? Despite the press that made serial killers seem commonplace, they weren't all that common. And it seemed unbelievable that one would be in residence in the tiny, safe town where she had lived all her life.

Her thoughts turned to Riley and the crimes that had brought the two of them together. As tired as she was, her mind whirled with what she knew of both crimes. Despite what Glen thought to the contrary, she believed they were connected.

"If it looks like a duck and quacks like a duck...it's a duck," she murmured to herself as she pulled into the parking lot of her apartment housing.

She felt it in her gut, in every fiber of her being. The person who killed Riley's father was also responsible for attempting to kill hers. Whatever had happened to his mother had also happened to hers.

Had it happened to others? Before this moment she hadn't considered the possibility that perhaps she and

Riley weren't the only ones whose lives had been ripped apart by this person or persons.

She was so tired it was difficult to even contemplate how they would go about checking into such a thing. Unfortunately, the Cherokee Corners Police Station didn't have the budget to have computers hooked into big mainframes and systems to exchange information.

Every year the police department requested a tax increase to help update and every year the voters turned them down. The area was depressed and people were eking out a living as best as they could. The last thing they wanted was more tax dollars leaving their pockets.

Most of the officers who used computers worked on laptops they had purchased themselves.

If she was going to check to see if there were other crimes like hers and Riley's, then she would need some help. It would require hours of time checking newspapers around the area, and with a brand-new murder investigation on her hands, she wouldn't have hours of extra time.

Riley would help. She'd call him later...after she got a couple hours of sleep. As she got out of her car, she looked up, the beauty of the sky overhead filling her with an ache of anguish.

Where are you, Mom? her heart cried. Are you someplace where you can see the sunrise? Are you cold? Hungry? She couldn't stand the thought of her mother suffering. Wherever you are, hang on, Mom.

We'll find you. I swear, we'll do everything in our power to find you.

She headed inside for some much-needed sleep.

Rita Birdsong James felt as if she were swimming up from the depths of a cotton-filled lake. Consciousness came and went, like streaks of lightning in a blackened sky. She fought for the surface of the lake. An urgency filled her brain, but somehow didn't transmit to the rest of her body.

Something was wrong…but what? She willed her eyes to open despite the fact that she felt the darkness pressing in around her, attempting to take her back to the bottom of the lake.

Her eyes opened, but it took a moment to adjust to her fuzzy vision. She was in bed, the color and pattern of the spread achingly familiar. Her bed. The illumination in the room came from the Tiffany-style lamp that was also familiar. Her lamp.

Her hand moved to the side of the bed next to her. Empty. But that wasn't unusual. Thomas always rose earlier than her. Any minute now he'd come in to wake her, carrying her first cup of coffee for the morning.

She smiled and her eyes drifted closed, the sense of urgency dissipating. All was well. She was in her own bedroom, in her own home. She was just tired…so very tired. She allowed the darkness to reclaim her.

Chapter 9

Riley hadn't expected to hear from Savannah again, not after he'd done such an incredibly stupid thing the night before. What had he been thinking by trying to pressure her into making him such a promise?

He stared out his trailer window where his crews were out in full force, clearing lots and preparing for new building sites.

What had he been thinking? He'd been thinking of her clinging to a bridge, staring into the waters below and considering joining her dead husband in some insane pact of undying love.

He'd been thinking of a world where Savannah Tallfeather no longer existed, where her heart would no longer beat, and it had frightened him.

It also frightened him just a little bit how much he wanted to be a part of her life, how jealous he was of a man named Jimmy who had died a watery death far before his time.

Amazing, really, how in the brief period he'd known her he felt so connected to her. At first he'd thought it was because they'd both shared the same experiences, the same grief because of the crimes that had shaken up their worlds.

He'd believed that this connection had created a sort of false intimacy between them. But with each moment that he spent with her, he realized there was absolutely nothing false about it.

Something about her resonated inside him, touched him as no woman ever had before. He wanted to see her happy. He wanted to see the darkness in her eyes dissipate. He wanted to be around when she redis-covered that life had possibilities.

It was just before five when she called, and he sat up straighter in his chair at the sound of her sweet, familiar voice.

"I heard you had a rough night," he said.

"How did you hear? It didn't make the morning papers."

"Scott."

"Ah, the mouth of Oklahoma," she said dryly.

"Cut him some slack," Riley said with a chuckle. "He means well."

"I only have a minute to talk. I've got to get back to the station, but I was wondering if you'd like to come to a birthday party tomorrow? My niece, Maggie, is turning six and despite all that's going on, Breanna is throwing her a little party."

He was both surprised and thrilled by her invitation. "Sure, I'd love to join you. Just let me know where and when." He quickly jotted down the address and the time she gave him.

"I have to warn you," she said. "I intend to ply you with cake and ice cream, then ask a favor of you."

"You don't have to ply me with anything. If you need a favor, just ask me."

"I'll talk to you about it tomorrow. I really don't have time now. I'm running in a hundred different directions with this new murder case. I'll see you tomorrow, Riley." Before he could say anything else the line went dead.

It was ridiculous how pleased he was that she had invited him to a birthday party, especially given the fact that she'd indicated part of the reason for inviting him was to ask a favor.

But she could have asked him a favor over the phone, or if she wanted to ask in person she could have met him in a restaurant. Instead she had invited him to a family gathering and that somehow felt like a big step forward in their relationship, such as it was.

He was surprised by how nervous he was the next day when he pulled up in front of an attractive two-story Victorian house with a big shady tree in the front yard. He checked the address he'd written down against the numbers on the house. They matched.

Savannah's car wasn't there yet and he wasn't sure if he should go ahead and knock on the front door or not. There were several other cars in the driveway, but he decided to sit and wait for Savannah's arrival.

A gaily-wrapped package sat on the passenger seat. He'd stopped in a toy store earlier in the day and had instantly been overwhelmed by the choices presented to him. Gadgets and gizmos, games and craft kits, it seemed the choices were endless.

He'd decided a doll would be appropriate for a six-year-old girl. But even then the selection was huge. There were dolls that sang and dolls that danced. There were dolls that swam and roller-skated and discoed and said prayers. He'd finally settled on a sweet-faced baby doll that did nothing.

From the time she'd called him the day before until now, he'd wondered what kind of favor she could possibly want from him. Maybe she and Clay wanted to go through his parents' house again? If that were the case, of course he'd allow them access.

He grabbed his gift and got out of the car as Savannah pulled in behind him and parked. His heart gave a little jump as she got out of the car, looking as cool and fresh as a stick of spearmint in a pastel-green sundress.

She carried a smaller gift in her hand and immediately pointed to the one he carried. ''You didn't have to do that,'' she exclaimed.

''Of course I did,'' he replied. ''I can't show up at a little girl's birthday party without a present. It would be positively un-American.''

She smiled and again his heart did a little flip-flop

in his chest. It wasn't the full, joyous smile he longed to see from her, but it was enough for the moment.

"How's Happy adjusting to life with a cop?" he asked as they headed toward the front door.

"Fine. She's already shredded two pairs of my panty hose and turned over a plant, so I've placed her under house arrest. She's also won my heart completely."

"I claim no responsibility for the damage wrought by my gift to you," he said.

Again she smiled. "I don't expect you to." Her smile faded as they reached the door. "Riley, this might be a little difficult...the party. It's the first gathering we've ever had where Mom and Dad aren't there."

"Hopefully it will be the last without them."

"I hope so," she said fervently. "And thanks for coming today." She hesitated a moment. "I didn't really want to come alone."

"I'm honored to be here."

She nodded, then knocked on the door. A pretty little girl with long brown hair and beautiful gray eyes opened the door. With a squeal of delight, she launched herself into Savannah's arms. "Aunt Savannah, I'm so glad you came to my party."

"I wouldn't have missed it for the world," Savannah exclaimed as she hugged the little girl. "And I brought a friend with me to your party. His name is Riley."

"Hi, Maggie," Riley said.

"Hi." She gazed at him with the open curiosity of a child. "Are you my Aunt Savannah's boyfriend?"

Savannah coughed in surprise, and Riley rocked back on his heels. "Well, let's see, I'm her friend and I'm a boy, so I guess I could be considered a boyfriend."

"That's nice," Maggie said, and at the same time Breanna appeared behind her daughter.

"Hi." She smiled warmly at her sister, then turned her smile on Riley. "You must be Riley. My sister has told me all about you. Please…come in."

As Riley followed the women inside, he wondered what Savannah had told her sister about him. Had she merely mentioned that he was a fellow victim of a crime or had she told him that that she liked him…that they had shared a soul-searing kiss? Did sisters exchange information like that?

The backyard was filled with squealing children and adults huddled in groups as if in defense of their offspring. Brightly colored balloon bouquets were tied to chairs and the picnic table held a huge cake decorated with white and pink icing and sugar candies in a variety of shapes.

Savannah led him to a group of people and introduced him to Adam, her brother-in-law, the infamous Uncle Sammy, and several other men who were apparently friends of the family.

It was an hour into the party before Riley began to successfully put faces to names.

As the children played games, the adults visited with one another. The talk was fairly benign…the weather, a new movie playing at the one theater in town, local politics. Riley spent much of his time watching Savannah.

He liked watching her interact with her sister. It was obvious the two were close and it was also obvious Savannah adored her niece.

Sammy James proved to be entertaining, regaling Riley with tales of travel and women and fortunes made and lost. He seemed bigger than life, devoted to his brother and sister-in-law and just a bit too slick for Riley.

Clay showed up late and distracted. He stayed only long enough to give Maggie his present, then left, murmuring that he was in the middle of processing the evidence from the latest murder scene.

Riley visited a little with Jacob Kincaid, the local banker in town, then spent some time talking to an older policeman named Charlie Smitherspoon. Charlie seemed genuinely upset by what had happened to the James family, but had few kind words to say about Thomas James.

"I ran against him for chief of police years ago, but he had it easy. He got all the Irish Catholics in town to vote for him, and his wife got all the Injuns to vote for him, too. I didn't have a chance."

Riley's blood heated but before he could comment to the man, Savannah touched his arm and motioned him to join her away from the crowd. She held two paper plates with a generous slice of cake on each.

"Have you checked out that man's alibi for the

night your father was hurt?" he asked as he took one of the plates for her.

"Why? Because he's an old, prejudiced moron? This town and the police department are full of men just like him. They think we Native Americans should go back to the reservation and sell beads and drink whiskey."

He looked at her in amazement. "How do you work with people who think like that?"

"I mostly ignore them." She gestured toward a pair of lawn chairs and they sat. "It's really not so bad. It's mostly the old-timers who are the most prejudiced. The younger guys don't have the same problems."

"Well, old Charlie there definitely seems to have a problem with your father."

"Charlie has never hidden the fact that he and my father didn't get along. Besides, if Charlie is responsible for what happened to my parents, then we have to consider that he's responsible for what happened to yours." She paused a moment and took a bite of her cake, leaving behind a tiny smudge of white frosting right next to her luscious upper lip.

Riley wanted to lean forward and clean it off with his mouth, swirl his tongue across her upper lip. He could almost taste the sugary sweetness coupled with the fiery heat of her mouth.

He'd been on a slow simmer all day where she was concerned. Watching her in that mint-colored sundress that exposed the length of her long, shapely legs and emphasized her slender waist and rounded breasts had stirred an undeniable desire in him.

He was like an adolescent, mortified more than once in the afternoon to find his body reacting to his wayward thoughts.

He focused his attention toward the children, who were playing a game of pin the tail on the donkey under the supervision of Breanna and Adam. "Thanks for inviting me here, Savannah," he said. "Birthday parties are always fun."

"When is your birthday, Riley?"

"September twenty-second." She frowned thoughtfully "What what's wrong?"

"I was just thinking. You mentioned that you have no family since your parents...since that night. So, who celebrates your birthday with you?"

That she would even think of such a thing touched him deeply. "You know, you get to be a certain age and it's just another day. Your niece is a cutie," he said to change the subject.

She looked at him for a long moment, then nodded. "Yes, she is. She gave us quite a scare a couple of months ago."

He looked back at her. "How so?"

"You know Breanna works vice, and usually on the weekends she works a prostitution detail. One of the men she had arrested for solicitation kidnapped Maggie. Thankfully we got her back quickly, safe and sound, and the perp is facing lots of time in prison."

"Your family has definitely been through the wringer."

She nodded, her eyes darkening. "And I hope both of my parents are at the next family gathering. Just like I hope we find your mother alive and well."

"Have you decided that you definitely think the same person is responsible for what happened to my family and what happened to yours? Did Clay find something to tie the two together?" He tried to focus on the conversation as she took another bite of her cake and found the errant smudge with the tip of her tongue.

"No, he hasn't finished with his tests to conclude that the two scenes are connected by forensic evidence. But, working this new murder scene made a thought come into my head. We're all hoping that Greg Maxwell and Sam McClane were killed by the same person, a person with a specific motive in mind, because if these were two random killings, it's a whole different ball game."

"You mean a serial killer." He took a bite of his cake to distract him from his intense desire to kiss her.

She nodded. "And thinking about a serial killer made me think about what happened to us." She set her cake down on her lap and gazed at him, her pretty brown eyes somber. "We know what happened at my parents' house and we know what happened at your parents' house two years ago. What we don't know is if these are the only two crimes like this."

All other thoughts fled from his brain as he realized the implication of her words. More? Was it possible there were more families where the fathers had been hurt or killed and the mothers had vanished?

He set his paper plate down, his appetite gone. "That's a horrible thought," he said as he pulled his chair closer to hers.

"I know." She rubbed the center of her forehead, her shoulders slumping slightly. "The problem is we don't have a computer geared to make the search easy, and it's going to require a major time commitment to find out, one that I can't make right now with this new murder on my plate."

"And that's where I come in," he said.

She frowned. "I hate to even ask, but if you have a computer and could do a little research...maybe make some phone calls."

"Why do you hate to ask?" He reached out and took her hand, finding it impossible not to touch her in some way. "We're in this together, Savannah, and I'll do whatever I can to help you find the people responsible."

For a moment he thought she was going to pull her hand away, but instead she twined her fingers with his and squeezed, and in that instant Riley knew that he was falling in love with Savannah Tallfeather.

"Tahlequah, Muskogee, Locust Grove..."

Savannah fought a rambunctious Happy as she tried to scribble down the names of cities and towns Riley reeled off.

"Wait a minute...what was that last one?" she

asked, and squeezed the phone receiver tighter against her ear.

It was late, after eleven, and Savannah was in bed, papers strewn everywhere around her. The phone calls from Riley had become a ritual for the past three nights, ever since she'd told him what she needed from him at the birthday party.

While she spent her days interviewing Sam Mc-Clane's family and friends and revisiting the Greg Maxwell files, he surfed the Internet, looking for crimes that were similar in nature to theirs.

Each night he called her with the names of the cities he'd checked, either through newspaper searches or by phone calls to the various police departments. So far their search had yielded nothing.

"That's it for today," he said.

Savannah set her pen down and relaxed against the pillows, fighting the bone-deep exhaustion that had become so familiar.

"So, how was your day?" he asked.

This was the part of their nightly conversations she'd come to anticipate the most…when they shared the details, often mundane details, of their day. There was something nice about having this just-before-she-fell-asleep contact with another caring human being.

"Frustrating," she replied. "The problem with a small town is there are too many links between victims. We have one barber, so Sam and Greg got their hair cut at the same place. Jacob Kincaid has the only bank in town so the two men banked at the same establishment…and so on…and so on." She snatched her pen from Happy's paws. "How about you? Did you have a good day?"

"Yeah, actually I did. Two families went to contract on two of my homes. Lillian brought blueberry muffins this morning instead of bran, and the last person I'm talking to before I go to sleep is you. Life is good."

A pleasant warmth washed over her at his words. She wondered if, like her, he was in bed. Was he naked beneath the sheets? A vision unfolded in her head, a vision of his tanned body against white sheets. As the warmth of her body intensified, she imagined she could smell him, that provocative fresh male scent.

"Savannah...did you fall asleep on me?" His deep voice vanquished the vision.

"No...I'm here. I'm glad you had a good day."

"What are your plans for tomorrow? It's your day off, isn't it?"

"Yes, but I think I'm going to go ahead and work. If I stall on the murder investigations, I can always do a little investigating on my parents' case."

"Has Glen okayed that?"

"He's given me permission to see the reports being generated, but I'm not to actively pursue the case." She tried to stifle a noisy yawn, but was unsuccessful.

"You're exhausted. Why don't you just take the day off tomorrow and give yourself a break?"

She didn't want downtime. She needed to keep going...pushing...searching. She needed activity. She didn't want time to think because lately when she did take a moment to think, her thoughts were as troubling as the events that had shaken up her life.

"I'll tell you what," he continued before she had a chance to reply. "Be ready at noon tomorrow. I'll pick you up."

She started to protest, then changed her mind. "Okay…but, be ready for what?"

"Be ready for anything. I'll see you at noon." He clicked off, leaving Savannah with a rush of sweet anticipation that she refused to even try to analyze.

She slept indecently late the next morning, waking only when Happy batted her in the head and mewled plaintively for breakfast.

At noon she stood in her living room looking out the front window, watching for Riley's arrival. The thoughts she'd been running away from for the past week came back in a rush to haunt her.

She liked Riley. She liked spending time with him. She liked the way his skin crinkled around his eyes when he smiled, when he laughed.

She walked over to the coffee table that held an array of photos. Her gaze lingered on one in particular. It was of Jimmy, his cheeks ruddy from the cold, and the fur of a parka framing his face.

She'd taken the picture on a wintry day just before his death. He'd protested that he looked like a polar bear in his jacket, but she insisted on taking the picture anyway. It had been the last photo she'd taken of him.

A wave of grief washed over her and she embraced it like a warm, familiar shawl. Unlike the emotions

Riley stirred in her, this emotion was oddly comforting.

For months her mother had tried to talk her into packing the photos away. "How can you move on when you keep the past staring you in the face all the time?" she'd said.

And now her mother was gone as well as Jimmy.

But, it wasn't the same, she quickly reminded herself. Jimmy was never coming back, but her mother was. Savannah had to keep the faith and believe it was true—it was just a matter of time before her mother returned to them. To even entertain thoughts to the contrary was impossible to bear.

She looked at the picture of Jimmy one last time, then turned away and went back to the window to watch for Riley. Just one day, she mentally told her husband. It's just one day with Riley.

It doesn't mean anything at all. It can never mean anything. You were my soul mate, Jimmy, and nothing will ever take away from my love for you.

Riley and I have things to discuss…things about the crime. That's all it is. She closed her eyes and allowed herself another moment to wallow in the familiar grasp of grief.

When she opened her eyes again and looked out the window, she saw Riley's truck pulling into the complex. She watched him park and get out of the truck. As he approached her door, all thoughts of Jimmy seeped out of her mind.

Riley looked so handsome. He was dressed casually in a pair of jeans. His short-sleeved white shirt was open at the collar and tucked into his jeans, emphasizing his slender waist and lean hips.

She smoothed a hand down her denim sundress, a flutter of crazy nervous anxiety rippling through her. What did he have planned for the day? He'd said to be ready for anything.

He spied her through the window and his lips curved into a smile that shot a river of warmth through her. And in that moment she knew she was—she was ready for anything.

Chapter 10

"Are you hungry?" Riley asked as he headed his truck out of town. He tried to keep his eyes on the road, but it was difficult when all he wanted to do was gaze at her.

She looked so pretty in her denim sundress, with her cinnamon-colored shoulders and long legs bare. She smelled as pretty as she looked, and he tightened his grip on the steering wheel, willing himself not to think about how much he wished he could kiss her again.

"Not really. I had a late breakfast. So, where are we going?" she asked curiously.

"I'm being self-indulgent and taking you to my dream."

"Ah, Riley Estates." She settled back in the seat, appearing relaxed.

"Actually, I have several things planned for the day," he said. "And there's only one rule."

"What's that?"

"I think we should make a deal that we aren't going to talk about murders or missing mothers or crimes of any kind. We are not going to talk about Internet searches or anything else that makes us feel bad or sad. What do you say? Is it a deal?"

"Sure, but that doesn't leave us much to talk about."

He flashed her a look of incredulity. "Savannah, we aren't the sum total of the crimes that happened to us. We'll find lots of things to talk about."

She nodded, a small smile curving her lips. "All right. I'm game if you are."

"Good." Riley's main concern today was giving her a day off, some time where she wasn't thinking about or working a case.

Each night that he'd spoken with her by phone he'd been struck by how tired she sounded and he'd known it wasn't a physical tiredness, but rather a mental exhaustion. He wanted to take her cares away, if only for this day.

"I spoke with Breanna this morning. She told me Maggie has named the doll you gave her Rose."

"Rose is a nice name. You like roses?" he asked.

She smiled again, that little smile that was merely a flirtatious hint of the kind of smile her lips were capable of. "What woman doesn't? However, my absolute favorite flower is black-eyed Susans...I think because my father used to call me black-eyed Savannah which always made my mother mad because she said if he was going to call me a nickname it should be my Cherokee name.''

"And what's that?'' he asked curiously.

She grinned teasingly. "Ah, I can't tell you. It's a Cherokee taboo to tell anyone your Native American name. If I told you, then I'd have to kill you.''

"Really?''

She laughed. "No, I just made that up.'' Her laughter died and she eyed him thoughtfully. "But I don't think I'm ready to tell you my Cherokee name yet.''

"Okay,'' he agreed. This was a side of Savannah he hadn't seen before. The coy teasing, almost flirtatious banter intensified his desire for more from her. "But, I won't be happy until I know your Cherokee name,'' he warned.

The drive to Sycamore Ridge seemed to take no time as they talked about all kinds of things. It was amazing how much they found to talk about, even without the mention of what he'd announced off-limits.

She spoke about some of the Cherokee traditions, enlightening him on a culture that was steeped in beautiful beliefs and ideals. It was obvious she was proud of her heritage, and he found himself wanting to learn more.

Although they had agreed not to discuss their mothers, she told him about Rita's work at the Cherokee Cultural Center and how that had been such a big part of Savannah's childhood.

By the time they reached the entrance to Riley Estates, he could tell she was more relaxed than he'd ever seen her. Her smile came frequently, and the tiny stress lines that had wrinkled her forehead seemed to have magically disappeared.

"Oh, Riley," she said as they drove through the entrance. "This is quite impressive."

Pride swelled inside him. "We still have a lot of landscaping to do around the entrance," he explained. "I want shrubs and flowers everywhere...you know, to add warmth." He parked in the driveway of one of the model homes, then smiled at her. "How about I give you the dollar tour?"

"Sounds nice," she replied.

For the next hour Riley led her around his dream. He showed her where the swimming pool would eventually be, where he intended to place a central park area. They went in and out of the model homes, climbed on equipment to see into the distance, hiked until they both were near exhaustion, then he took her to his office to meet Lillian.

"It's so nice to meet you," Lillian said as she motioned Savannah into one of the chairs in Riley's office. "Riley has spoken so highly of you. Iced tea...that's what we need. You both look parched. I suppose he had you traipsing all over the countryside."

She disappeared from the office and a small giggle escaped Savannah. Riley grinned. "Hard to get a word in edgewise when she gets going."

"She seems quite sweet."

"She is," Riley replied. "I'm not sure what I would have done without her the past six months."

"You would have done just fine," Lillian said as she reentered the office carrying two tall glasses of tea. "But, you wouldn't be as organized and you definitely wouldn't be eating enough fiber."

She handed Savannah a glass of the tea and smiled. "Nobody realizes just how important fiber is to the diet. Let me know if you two need anything else," she said to Riley, then left the office once again and closed the door behind her.

Riley sat in the chair behind his desk and grinned at Savannah, then took a deep drink of the iced tea. "And this…is my world," he said as he set the glass down on his desk.

"And a nice world it is," she replied. "I can't imagine anything nicer than being a builder, knowing that each house you build will be a family's home, the place where they live and dream and love."

She got it. She got his dream. "A lot of people assume builders go into their trade for the money and there's no denying that if you are successful there's plenty of money to be had with building homes."

She took a sip of her tea, then smiled at him. The warmth of her smile eddied through him. "But, that's not the reason why you do it, is it?" She stood and walked over to the window and peered out. "Your vision here isn't about money. It's about people." She turned back to face him.

He'd never wanted to kiss a woman as much as he wanted to kiss her at that moment. He wanted to take her into his arms, feel her warm curves against him as his mouth explored hers. In truth, he wanted to do far more than kiss her.

He cleared his throat, fighting against the desire that simmered in his veins. "You hungry?" he asked.

She nodded. "Starving."

"Me, too." He got up from his desk. "Let's go get something to eat." They finished their tea, said goodbye to Lillian, then got back into Riley's truck.

"So, where are we eating?" she asked.

"Chez Riley's." He cast a quick glance in her direction. "I thought I'd take you to my place, let you see where I live and where a meal fit for a king is waiting for us."

"Really? You cooked?"

He grinned sheepishly. "Actually, to be perfectly honest, I shopped." He hesitated a beat. "Little Doe?"

"Excuse me?"

"Just making a guess about your Cherokee name," he said.

She laughed. "Little Doe? Couldn't you at least be a little original?"

"Okay…Foolish Fawn," he teased.

Her laughter rang in the truck and he relished the sound of it. He wanted to make her laugh always, to see that glimmer of happiness shine in her eyes every day of his life.

"Not even close," she exclaimed. She grew silent as he pulled into his driveway. He shut off his motor and turned to look at her. "It's beautiful, Riley. Absolutely beautiful, and the setting is stunning."

He looked back at the house. It was a beautiful place, and there wasn't another house in sight, only trees and grass and carefully planted shrubbery. "Thanks."

They got out of the car and he led her inside, and as he saw the living room through her eyes he realized his mother had been right. It was a beautiful house, but it wasn't a home, and he felt the need to apologize for the cold, impersonal living conditions.

"I'm not here much. The place needs a little TLC."

She walked across the living room and stood before the floor-to-ceiling windows that offered a scenic view of a small brook and ancient trees. "Why hang pictures and put out knickknacks in a house that offers this kind of view?"

He came to stand just behind her, drawing a deep breath of the scent of her. "It is beautiful, isn't it?" He pointed to a spot down by the brook. "That's where we're going to eat our dinner."

"How wonderful." She turned to look at him and they were so close he could feel her breath on his face. Time seemed to come to a halt as they stood face-to-face, a mere breath apart.

Every muscle in his body tensed as desire rocked him nearly mindless. He wanted to back her up against the window, claim her lips with his while his hands caressed up the length of her legs, up beneath her denim skirt. He wanted to press himself against her, let her feel the extent of his need for her.

Her eyes widened, as if she could read his thoughts, see inside his head and into his deepest desire. "When...when do we eat?"

He saw her mouth move, and somewhere in the back of his brain the words registered, but her voice sounded very faraway and huskier than usual.

"Riley?"

The moment shattered as Riley heard the apprehension in her voice. "Now," he said as he stepped back from her. "Now we eat."

The picnic basket he'd prepared earlier was in the refrigerator, all packed and ready to go. He handed her a neatly folded red blanket then he grabbed the basket and the jug of cold sweet tea and they headed outside.

It was a perfect evening for a picnic, warm but with a slight breeze that made the temperature comfortable. "How did you find this property?" she asked as they spread the blanket out in the lush grass.

"It was part of a ranch that belonged to a friend of my father's. He couldn't use this area for planting because it was too wooded so he sold me these three acres."

"It's beautiful," she exclaimed.

No, you are, he thought. You're beautiful and sexy and have me half-crazy with wanting you.

They both sat on the blanket and he opened the picnic basket. He was hungry, but the last thing he hungered for was food.

* * *

As they ate, Riley entertained her with stories about his job. He told her about temperamental workers, small-time thugs and crazy prospective home buyers.

He made her laugh again and again and she realized how desperately she'd needed this day away from the strife, the worry and the very torment of her life.

He made it impossible for her to think of anything but him and this moment of laughter and good food. He made it impossible for her to regret the impulse that had made her accept his invitation for the day.

Dinner consisted of what he'd once told her made a perfect picnic meal—thick ham sandwiches, potato salad and chips, and for dessert, big slices of chocolate cake.

As they talked and ate, evening shadows danced first around the base of the trees, then spread to embrace all they could find.

Savannah ate too much, and as Riley finished his meal, she stretched out on the blanket, a languid sense of well-being seeping through her. The nearby brook made little bubbling noises as it cascaded over rocks. The sound was almost hypnotically soothing.

She didn't realize she'd gone to sleep until she opened her eyes to discover the sun had fallen from the sky and the moon had taken its place. Riley was stretched out beside her, propped up on his elbow, watching her.

''Oh, goodness. I'm sorry,'' she exclaimed. She propped herself up on her elbow facing him, embarrassed that she'd apparently slept for a little while. "I didn't mean to fall asleep."

"Don't apologize," he said with a smile. "You were obviously exhausted."

"It was all that good food you provided," she replied. "And the sound of the little stream." She knew she should sit up, tell him it was time to take her home, but she was reluctant to call an end to what had been a near-perfect day.

Besides, he looked so handsome in the purple shadows of night. His blue eyes glowed with an almost silvery sheen and the bright moonlight that streamed through the trees emphasized the chiseled planes of his face.

"Thank you, Riley, for a wonderful day," she said softly.

"No. Thank you," he returned. "I can't remember a day that I've found more pleasurable." The glow in his eyes seemed to intensify and he reached out a hand and stroked a strand of her short hair away from her forehead.

"I like your hair short," he said softly. "It draws attention to your beautiful face. And you are so beautiful," he murmured.

He didn't pull his hand away from her, but rather it lingered, touching her cheek, tracing down the line of her jaw.

She could feel it in the air; her senses were taut with it. Desire. It shone from his eyes, radiated from his touch and welled up inside of her. She knew he was going to kiss her and for the life of her she couldn't imagine telling him no.

He leaned forward and she met him halfway. His warm mouth moved against hers with featherlight softness, but the softness lasted only a moment before his mouth became more demanding.

She gave in to the kiss, opening her mouth to him as his tongue met hers. He was no longer inches away from her, but rather pressed against her, his arms gathering her closer...closer against him.

It felt good, to be held intimately against the length of him, her softness against his strength, her heat melding with his. The kiss went on and she reveled in the taste of him, the hot demand that was in his lips.

She tangled her hands in his hair, loving the feel of it between her fingers. Her heart pounded a rhythm to match the beat of his...racing...almost frantic.

His mouth left hers and trailed a hot rain of kisses down her jaw, then behind her ear. The sweet sensations forced a shiver of need to work through her.

She felt his fingers behind her working at the zipper of her sundress and she didn't want to stop, knew they were both beyond stopping. Her need for this human contact was too great and she wanted Riley, the man who made her laugh, the man who seemed to understand her from the inside out.

Hunger thrummed in her veins, crashed in her heart. She didn't want to think. She only wanted to feel...experience making love with Riley.

"Savannah," he whispered, his voice no louder

than the babble of the nearby brook. "Sweet Savannah…" Her zipper hissed down and he pulled her to a sitting position. The opened dress fell from her shoulders and she got to her feet, letting it fall to the blanket.

At the same time he stood and kicked off his jeans, then yanked his shirt open and tore it off. Together they fell back on the blanket, guided by a frenzied need and in no time at all they both were naked.

There was a surreal feeling to the whole thing…the night air coupled with moonlight splashed their bodies. She'd never made love outside before, and there was a part of her that marveled at the abandon she felt, the utter freedom of it all.

Her head was filled not only with the male scent of Riley, but also with the sweet smell of grass, the rich fragrance of earth and the hint of woodsy wildness. She felt as wild as the landscape that surrounded them…as soft as the grass, as liquid as the stream, as warm as the ground that retained the day's sunshine.

He stroked her skin, his hands feeling fevered as they cupped her breasts, caressed down the length of her stomach, and smoothed across the tops of her thighs.

She wanted to weep with pleasure and scream at him to take her. She didn't want foreplay. She'd been ready for him since the moment of their first kiss.

"Riley," she finally managed to gasp. And that was all it took to snap whatever control he'd fought to maintain. He entered her in one smooth thrust and groaned as he remained unmoving, buried completely inside her.

She raked her fingers down his bare back and with another groan he moved his hips against hers. And in that moment they were at each other like hungry animals. Only their gasps and moans, their ragged breaths and groans, broke the silence of the night.

Almost as quickly as it had begun, it was finished. They fell apart, each trying to catch their breaths. Rational thought was still impossible for Savannah. She was a bundle of feelings, overwhelmed by sweet sensations, and in any case she didn't want to think—not yct.

He reached out and drew a finger down her cheek, his eyes glowing in the moonlight overhead. "You are so beautiful, Savannah." His voice held a softness that touched her deep inside.

"Silver Star," she said. He frowned quizzically. "My Cherokee name is Silver Star."

He smiled. "That would have been my next guess." His smile faded as he continued to look at her. "I'm sorry it was, uh, so fast."

A wave of heat suffused her face. "It was fine, Riley."

His frown deepened. "Only fine?"

"More than fine...wonderful." She was completely embarrassed now. She sat up and reached for her panties and bra.

"I never even gave you the whole tour of my house," he said as they dressed.

She was grateful for the change in subject. "I'd love to see the rest of your house."

Together they picked up the last of the picnic things and the blanket, then went back into his house. As he put on a pot of coffee, she excused herself to go to the bathroom.

In the privacy of the guest bath, she stared at her reflection in the mirror. Her cheeks were pink and her eyes sparkled and her lips were slightly swollen and red.

They'd been like two animals going at each other, she thought. It had been all about physical need, and somehow that comforted her. Her body had responded, but of course her heart hadn't been involved at all.

When she left the bathroom and returned to the kitchen she was grateful that they suffered no apparent awkwardness between them.

They drank coffee and he told her about building his house. "I'm grateful that my parents were here to see this completed and me living here," he said.

"So you've been here a couple of years," she said in surprise. By the austere living room and kitchen, she would have guessed he'd moved in only a couple of months before.

"Yeah, hard to believe, isn't it? I keep telling myself maybe I should hire an interior decorator to kind of liven up the place, but so far I haven't managed to bring myself to do it." He hesitated a beat. "Maybe you could give me some ideas for making it seem more homey."

She laughed. "Trust me, I'm the last person to ask. My mother constantly tells me my taste is all in my mouth when it comes to decorating."

He stood from the table where they had been sitting. "Come on, let me give you the whole tour."

He took her upstairs first, where there was a large bath and three nice-size bedrooms. Each room had a bed and dresser, but nothing on the walls and no specific style at all.

"You know, you might check out Tamara Greystone's work. She does wonderful paintings that would perk up your walls a bit," she offered.

"Maybe you'd go with me to see some of her stuff...help me pick out some artwork."

"Sure," she agreed as he led her back down the stairs. "Although her work is so good you couldn't make a mistake in choosing any of it."

The dining room was attractive with an elegant table and chairs and a matching china cabinet. "You have wonderful taste," she said as she ran a finger across the polished wood of the table.

"Thanks." He touched her arm. "Come on, and I'll show you the master suite."

She wasn't sure why but the thought of seeing where Riley slept, where he dreamed, filled her with a new tension, a strange, exciting tension.

The bedroom was huge and light and airy. The room held the essence of Riley Frazier. His scent hung in the air and photos of his parents in small gold frames stood on the top of the dresser, along with loose change and several sheets of paper containing doodles.

The bed was king-size and covered with a dark-blue spread and burgundy throw pillows. The curtains carried out the same color scheme, looking rich and masculine. The windows offered the same view as the living room windows—that of the brook and the trees and the utter serenity of the property.

"It's beautiful, Riley," she said. She couldn't imagine the pleasure of waking up each morning with that view in sight. How peaceful it must be.

She walked over to the photos on the dresser, aware of him coming to stand just behind her. Funny, how quickly her senses responded to his nearness.

She looked at a photo of him with his mother and father. He seemed to be about eighteen or nineteen and all of their faces shone with the happiness of love...of family togetherness.

"She's probably dead."

His words, spoken softly, shocked and horrified her. She whirled around to face him, saw the stark despair on his features.

"Don't say that, Riley," she exclaimed. "Don't even think it."

"I need to face reality," he replied, his beautiful eyes dark with pain. "I have to face the fact that after all this time without a word, without a trace, she surely must be dead."

"No, you can't think that way." Savannah placed a hand on his cheek, felt the whisper of dark whiskers against her palm.

His words frightened her. If he truly believed there was no hope for his mother, then she had to face the possibility that there was no hope for hers.

"You have to keep the faith, Riley. Nobody has found her, there's been no body. You have to keep hoping, keep believing that eventually she'll be found alive and well."

He placed his hand over hers and closed his eyes for a moment, then nodded. "You're right. I've got to keep hoping."

She started to remove her hand, but he kept it pressed tightly against his cheek with his own. "Savannah." His voice was just a whisper, but it sent a shiver up her spine for it was filled with desire. "I want you again…here, in my bed."

"Riley, I…" She wasn't sure what she'd intended to say and in any case speech was impossible as his mouth crashed down on hers and all thoughts of protest were swept out of her head.

Chapter 11

The first time they had made love, it had been like two animals wanting only physical release, with little emotion, little tenderness involved. What Riley wanted now was to make love to her slowly... tenderly and with every ounce of emotion he had in his heart.

He turned off the overhead light and by the illumination of the moon drifting through the windows led her to the edge of the bed. Quickly he pulled down the bedspread, afraid that if he took too much time in preparing, she'd change her mind.

He turned back to her and gathered her in his arms. Willingly she came to him, her lips warm and yielding as he kissed her again and again. He felt as if he would never tire of kissing her, but knew eventually he'd want more...he'd want not just her lips, but all of her.

He cupped her face in his hands and stared deep into her eyes, seeing the glazed look of desire shining back at him. ''Savannah, I want you so badly.''

He fought for control, not wanting to lose it as quickly as he had earlier when they'd made love. He'd been almost embarrassed by his lack of control earlier.

''I want you, too,'' she whispered, as if the words caused her pain.

What he wanted was to take the time to know her, to explore each and every inch of her, to discover all the secrets that led to her passion.

Once again they undressed, then slid beneath the sheets. He was pleased to realize that long after she'd gone, his sheets would retain the scent of her, that indelible, unforgettable, delectable scent of warm sexy woman and sweet flowers.

As he claimed her lips again, his hands stroked down to capture her breasts. She had perfect breasts, not too big but not too small. As he rubbed his thumbs across her turgid nipples a deep moan issued from her throat. The moan shot fire through his veins, and he replaced his hands with his mouth, moving from one nipple to the other. She tasted so good and he loved the feel of her against his tongue.

Her hands clutched his shoulders and stroked his back, igniting tiny flames wherever she touched. His lips moved down her flat stomach as her fingers tangled in his hair.

He wanted to taste every inch of her, feel her writhe against him in mindless passion. He wanted to love her as she'd never been loved before, as she'd never be loved again.

Someplace in the back of his mind he knew he wanted to love her deeply enough, passionately enough to banish any thought, at least for the moment, of a man who could never, would never be in her life again.

Silver Star. Her Cherokee name sang through his head. She was like a shining silvery star in his heart, filling him with heat and light after years of darkness and despair.

Before this moment he'd only imagined what she would look like in his bed. Her dusky skin glistened in the moonlight, stoking his need for her to a near-fever pitch.

"Riley," she cried out as he found the center of her, stroked her with his hand, then with his mouth. It wasn't a cry of protest, but rather one of exquisite pleasure. Shudders racked her body, and only then did he move back up, raining kisses as he went.

Then it was her turn to explore his body and he trembled beneath the heat of her hands and the warmth of her mouth. She was a bold lover, matching him caress for caress, kiss for kiss.

"I love touching you…tasting you," he murmured into the hollow of her neck.

She stroked her hand up the hard length of him. "I love touching you, tasting you, too."

Once again his fingers found her warm moistness

and he saw her eyes widen as her hand fell away from him. As he moved his fingers against her, she clutched at the sheets, her hips rising to meet his as her body grew taut.

As she moaned her delight, he felt his own desire growing harder...higher...reaching heights he hadn't thought possible.

A series of shudders swept over her and he knew she was riding the crest of a tsunami that left her weak and gasping. It was only then, when he knew she'd had complete and total pleasure, that he entered her.

She wrapped her legs around his hips, bringing him into her completely at the same time his lips possessed hers in a fiery kiss of both dominance and submission.

Riley felt his control slipping. He was surrounded by her warmth, imbibed with her scent, and capable of only one single thought...Savannah...Savannah.

She sang inside him, heating his blood, permeating his veins, and filling up every corner of his heart. He loved her, and words of love begged to be released, but he had enough sense left to know it was too soon.

And so he loved her in every other way that he could, stroking her sweet skin, whispering sweet, loving words in her ear as he moved in and out of her.

As much as he wanted to take it slow, to make this act last forever, he couldn't. She was too much for him, too hot, too soft, too overwhelming to fight the natural impulse of his body to race to completion.

His movements became faster, but she met him thrust for thrust. Moans filled the room and he wasn't sure if they came from her or from him. All he knew was that he was lost...lost in Savannah, and he never wanted to be found again.

Afterward, he held her in his arms, unsure what to say. Making love to her had only confirmed what he had already known—that he loved her as he'd never loved a woman before, that he wanted to spend the rest of his life with her.

But he knew, more than anyone did, just how fragile she was, the turmoil of her life right now. Was she ready to welcome love? He wasn't sure and he was afraid of risking everything by moving too far too fast. They'd made beautiful love, but that didn't mean she was ready for a lifetime commitment.

"I've got to go," she said, breaking the silence that had lingered between them. "I've got a lot of things to do tomorrow."

He tightened his grip around her, reluctant to let her go. "Stay the night. I can take you home as early as you need in the morning." He'd love to wake up with her nestled in his arms. "There's nothing that can be accomplished tonight. Sleep here...with me."

She tensed, then pushed out of his arms and sat up. "No, I really need to go home now." She raked her fingers through her short hair, her gaze not meeting his. "If you don't feel like driving me home I can call a friend or a cab. It's no big deal."

"Don't be silly. Of course I'll take you."

She grabbed her clothes from the floor and disappeared into the master bathroom. Riley sat up and finger combed his hair, disappointment like a stone heavy in his chest.

He'd lost her. The closeness, the intimacy that had transcended a mere physical level had vanished. She'd distanced herself from him in the blink of an eye. He'd thought he'd known loneliness over the past two years, but in that instant he felt a loneliness he'd never experienced before.

Reluctantly, he got out of bed and turned on the bedside lamp. He would have loved to have her in his bed all night long. He would have loved to open his eyes with the sunrise and see her next to him.

But what he wanted didn't matter. He knew he had to be patient with her, and he had to find the patience within himself to give her time. They'd known each other for only two weeks. Although that was enough time for him to know his feelings for her, it was obviously not enough time for her.

He had just finished dressing when she came out of the bathroom. The first thing he saw on her face was regret. "Savannah...don't," he said softly.

"Don't what?" Still her gaze didn't quite meet his.

"No regrets," he said. "Please don't regret what happened here tonight." He took a step toward her. He wanted to reach out to her, take her in his arms. But he could tell by her posture and the shuttered look in her eyes that she wouldn't welcome any touch from him at the moment.

"I have no regrets," she said, but her body language said otherwise as she headed for the bedroom door. "I just have a lot on my mind."

Riley followed behind her, wondering how something that had been so beautiful, so moving, could have been a mistake. It was odd. He felt as if he was losing her and yet wasn't sure he'd ever really had her.

As Riley and Savannah got into his car, Rita Birdsong James came awake once again. Her head pounded with a headache the likes of which she'd never suffered before. The dim light from her nightstand only made it worse, and she closed her eyes and fought against the pain.

She reached out a hand to Thomas's side of the bed. "Thomas?" His side of the bed was cold. He'd always been an earlier riser than she had. Thomas loved the early mornings, and Rita didn't really come alive until midmorning.

Wincing, she opened her eyes once again. She had no idea what time it might be, felt the grogginess of too much deep sleep. Surely it was time to get up, but where was the sun?

Her gaze shifted toward her nightstand, searching for her clock radio, but it wasn't there. She frowned. That was odd. Why would her clock be gone? But her lamp was there, the Tiffany-style shade in reds and greens and deep blues.

She clutched a handful of the familiar bedspread, a flutter of disquiet coursing through her as she frowned and once again squeezed her eyes tightly closed. There was something…some nebulous memory just out of reach begging to come to the surface.

Her chest tightened and her headache intensified as she tried to think, but she felt as if her head had been stuffed with wads of cotton.

Maybe if she got up, opened the curtains and oriented herself as to the time of day. "Thomas?" she called as she carefully swung her legs over the edge of the bed.

Where was Thomas? The disquiet that had been with her moments before transformed into something deeper, more frightening.

Thomas. Something had happened to Thomas—but what? She managed to stand despite the fact that she felt weak and wobbly as a baby attempting first steps.

She clung to the nightstand for a moment, then stumbled to the curtains. Sunshine. Surely sunshine would make her feel better. Sunshine and a nice hot cup of coffee. Where was Thomas with the coffee?

She opened the drapes, but no sunshine greeted her. She stared uncomprehending at the concrete wall behind the curtains. Where was the window?

Jerking around, she looked at the room that she'd thought was her own. But now she saw that it wasn't really her room at all. It was a facade, like a set constructed for a play.

The bed was like hers, the bedspread exactly like the one she had in her room. The nightstand was the same, as was the lamp that sat on it. The walls were the same beige and the pictures hanging on the walls were very similar to the ones she owned. But, this wasn't her room.

Panic welled up inside her, a panic verging on

sheer hysteria. As the cotton in her head fell away, she moved away from the curtains, trying to get a handle on exactly where she might be.

It was a room made to look like hers, but there were no windows. A door led to a bathroom where there were fluffy towels on a shelf, her favorite scented powders and lotions on the countertop and her bathrobe, hung from a hook on the back of the door.

Was this a hospital? Certainly her head hurt badly enough for her to believe she'd been hospitalized. And somewhere in the dark places of her mind, she remembered being taken to the bathroom, being helped in and out of bed.

But what kind of a hospital provided rooms that looked almost exactly like the patient's bedroom at home?

There was another door, a strange steel door with what appeared to be a panel that could be opened and closed in the center. She made her way over to it and gripped the handle. Locked.

The instant she tried to turn the handle, the memory that had been niggling at her mind crashed open.

She'd been in the kitchen preparing to cut a piece of apple pie for Thomas when she'd heard him cry out. She'd smiled, thinking he was voicing his objection to a referee's call in the baseball game he'd been watching.

She'd just sliced the pie when she was grabbed from behind, and a large, gloved hand clamped across her nose and mouth. A strange smell burned her eyes, and she tried to hold her breath, fought desperately to get free. But darkness descended, and just before she lost total consciousness she caught a glimpse of Thomas sprawled facedown on the living room floor. Blood was everywhere...too much blood.

She now cried out and fell weakly to her knees as she thought of her beloved husband. ''Thomas... Thomas.'' She wept his name over and over again. He was dead. He had to be dead...there had been too much blood and he'd been so still.

Raven Mocker. That's who had come into their home and killed Thomas. Only Raven Mocker, the most evil of Cherokee witches, could be responsible.

She thought of all the stories her mother had told her about the dreadful Raven Mocker. According to the ancient stories, Raven Mocker flew through the night with his arms outstretched like wings and went into the house of somebody that was sick or dying and robbed them of their life.

But Raven Mocker was just a legend, like the Anglo bogeyman, her mind protested. Despite the fact that she was a modern woman, she couldn't deny the power of the stories she'd been told about the dreaded witch of her people.

Although she and Thomas were not ill, there was no doubt in her mind that only the evil Raven Mocker would be powerful enough, evil enough to kill Thomas and take her.

She rose to her feet and tried to open the door once again, but she couldn't. She made her way back to the bed and sat on the edge, fighting against the grief that threatened to rip her apart. Not only was she fighting her grief, but she also felt so very tired and realized she must have been drugged.

Shaking her head to try to get the fog out, she looked around the room once again and noticed the open closet. The clothing that hung inside was familiar. They were all hers...the dresses, the blouses, the skirts...all had hung in her closet at home.

What was going on here? What was happening? Her gaze darted frantically around the room. No windows—a locked steel door.

Raven Mocker had stolen Thomas's life and now held her as a prisoner. For what? Grief battled with terror and she curled up on the bed, wondering how long before she learned what her fate was to be.

He watched her on four screens, the images transmitted from the dozen cameras built into the ceiling of the room. Each screen gave him a different bird's-eye view and with the flick of a switch he could turn the camera's eyes so she would never be out of his view no matter where she was in the room.

She was weeping and he'd heard her cry her husband's name again and again. That was natural. He understood her grief and knew eventually it would pass.

He'd stopped the drugs, eager to see her awake and moving instead of inert and lifeless on the bed. He knew he'd have to tolerate her grief for several days to come, perhaps even a week or two, but if there was one thing he was, it was a patient man.

Soon she would come to understand that she belonged here...with him. She'd come to realize that she was special...a chosen one.

He hoped she didn't disappoint him.

He'd been disappointed so many times in the past.

"Good night, Riley," Savannah said and jumped out of his truck before he could even offer to walk her to her door. If he walked her to her door he'd want to kiss her good-night, and she was afraid a kiss from Riley at this moment would shatter her into a million pieces.

She hurried to her apartment door, unlocked it, then went inside and slammed the door shut behind her. She locked it again, then sagged weakly against it.

The drive home had been silent, filled with tension and for her, filled with regret. She'd made love with Riley not once, but twice. Once, she could chalk up to raging hormones or a lack of control. She could have told herself he'd seduced her, that she'd been weak and vulnerable and he'd taken advantage of her.

But no matter how hard she tried she couldn't excuse or explain away the second time. She'd gone willingly to his bed, wanting the pleasure of being naked and intimate with him between his sheets.

She had been a willing participant in their lovemaking—lovemaking that had gone beyond the boundaries of mere physical pleasure.

She pushed herself away from the front door and stepped into the living room where the photos of Jimmy seemed to stare at her in accusation.

Tears burned at her eyes and she raced into her bathroom, stripped off her clothes and got into the shower. She scrubbed herself in the near-scalding water, needing to remove every trace of Riley.

She only wished there was some way to take out her memories and rinse them clean of him, as well. But his smile remained in her head, the sound of his laughter rang in her ears, and the warm light of his eyes bathed her in a heat that had nothing to do with the shower water.

As she dried off and pulled on her nightgown, she thought of her mother. How Savannah wished her mother was here right now, to talk to, to hold her and make all the madness of her life go away.

From the bathroom she wandered back into the living room and picked up the frame with the photo of Jimmy in his parka. She curled up on the sofa with the photo in hand, staring at the man who had been friend, companion, lover and husband.

Life had been so easy when Jimmy had been with her. There had been no murders, no missing mother, no lonely nights and no torturous feelings of guilt.

His brown eyes were so gentle…so kind. But so were Riley's blue ones, a little voice whispered. Jimmy had made her laugh. Riley makes you laugh, too, the voice whispered.

And Riley had made her body sing as it never had before. He'd made her feel alive for the first time in over a year. Even now, just thinking about their lovemaking sent a shimmering wave of heat through her.

She grabbed the photo of Jimmy tighter and

clutched it against her chest. He'd been her destiny, her soul mate. She closed her eyes in an attempt to stanch the hot tears that threatened. But the attempt was futile, and tears spilled down her cheeks as she realized she couldn't remember her soul mate's kiss. Her head was too filled with Riley.

Chapter 12

She'd stopped taking his calls. Every night for the next three nights Riley called her at the same time, as had become their habit. And each night he got her answering machine. He suspected she was home, listening to his messages, but refusing to pick up and actually talk to him.

It killed him. After what they had shared, it killed him to know she was now attempting to push him right out of her life.

She was in love with him, he knew it in his heart. He knew she wasn't the kind of woman who could make love with somebody she didn't care about or wasn't falling in love with. Yes, he believed she was falling in love with him but was bound heart and soul to a dead man.

How could he ever hope to compete with a marriage that would never suffer any more discord, a marriage that would forever be happy in the memories of the woman left behind?

How could he ever hope to compete with a man who could now never disappoint or hurt her in any way?

The messages Riley had left for her had been lists of additional cities and towns where he'd checked records to see if he could find a case like theirs. So far there had been nothing, but in every minute of his spare time he got back on the Internet and the telephone to search some more.

That's what he was doing when his other phone line rang. He snatched it up, hoping, praying it was Savannah. But instead it was her brother, Clay.

"Found something interesting," he said without preamble.

"And what would that be?" Riley asked.

"Pebbles."

"Excuse me?" Riley shut down his computer to better focus on the conversation.

"Pebbles...little rocks. There were two in the carpeting at your parents' house and three in the carpeting at my folk's place."

Riley frowned, not understanding the significance. "I would expect there to be pebbles in everyone's carpeting. There are all kinds of rocks and gravel around."

"But not like these," Clay replied. "These aren't your garden variety pebbles. They're polished, decorative rocks used for landscaping."

"Can you tell where they come from? Who sells them?" Adrenaline pumped through him. Maybe finally...finally they had gotten a break in the cases.

"Unfortunately there are three rock quarries in this county that sell them and a dozen quarries throughout the state. I'm in the process now of requesting customer lists from all of them, but I'm not sure if we'll learn anything from them or not."

"So, we're back to square one," Riley said, fighting a wave of disappointment.

"Not exactly. I'd say with this evidence, it's possible that whoever killed your father also tried to kill mine."

"Possible, but you can't be certain."

There was a moment of silence and Riley felt the other man's frustration radiating across the line. "I couldn't testify in a court of law unequivocally that the two crimes were committed by the same person based on this evidence alone."

"But what do you think, Clay?" he pressed, wanting a definitive answer.

"I don't think. That's not my job. I analyze trace evidence. It's just intriguing, that's all, that the same kind of rock was found at both places. I thought you'd like to know."

"I appreciate it. Have you told Savannah?"

"Yeah. It was her idea that I call and let you know."

Riley's suspicion that Savannah was avoiding him was confirmed by Clay's words. A week ago there was no way in hell Savannah wouldn't have been on the phone to him to share this piece of news. But a week ago they hadn't made love.

He rebooted the computer and stared at the screen. How could making love to her screw everything up between them? He hadn't forced himself on her. She'd been a willing participant both times.

He'd never experienced the kind of pleasure he'd had making love to Savannah. It hadn't been just the act itself, but the beauty of looking deep into her eyes, feeling the beat of her heart against his, knowing a bond was being cemented between them that went beyond the mere physical act of lovemaking.

At least that's what he'd thought. He suspected he knew what had chased her away—the memories of a man now dead. Jimmy Tallfeather must have been a hell of a man to still have such a hold on his wife a year after his death.

Riley wanted to break that hold. He didn't want Savannah to forget the man she'd loved and married, but he wanted her to open her heart to the possibility that she could love and marry and be happy once again.

He shut off his computer, realizing it was impossible to work with her filling his every thought. Instead he decided to knock off from work altogether, take a ride into Cherokee Corners and see if he could find Savannah.

If he could just see her, speak with her in person, then he hoped he could convince her there was no reason to feel bad or guilty about what they had shared. He hoped he could convince her they belonged together.

"Lillian, I'm taking off for the rest of the afternoon," he said as he left his office.

"You might as well," she said. "You've been here all day, but you haven't been here, if you know what I mean." She tapped the side of her head to make her point. "If I was to guess, you've got woman problems," she added.

Riley smiled at her, surprised by her astuteness. On impulse he sat in the chair opposite her desk. "Lillian, you're a widow."

She nodded. "It's been five years since I lost my Joseph."

"And you've never remarried," he observed.

"That's true," she agreed. "What's with all these questions? Is this about your Savannah?"

Your Savannah. He loved the way that sounded and he desperately wanted to make it so. He hadn't realized until these last couple of weeks with her how utterly lonely, how desolate his life had become.

Before meeting Savannah he'd just been going through the motions, enduring each day without real pleasure. She'd changed all that for him. She'd filled his days with joy, given him a new hope for his future. She'd made him believe happiness was possible again despite the tremendous loss in his life.

"Riley?" Lillian looked at him expectantly.

"Sorry, yes it's about Savannah. Why haven't you remarried?" he asked.

Lillian blinked, as if finding it difficult to track the

conversation. "I don't know. I haven't met anyone since Joseph that has made me think of marrying again. I've grown accustomed to being alone and it's not like I *need* to remarry.

I have my gentlemen friends. I go to dinner or whatever, then send them on their way."

Riley frowned, trying to think what this might have to do with Savannah's widowhood.

"But you have to remember, Riley, I'm an old woman. I've had my children, I was married for thirty-five years."

"She clings to the memory of her husband, and I think she's refusing to even give us a chance. I respect the fact that she misses him, but I can't believe she intends to hold on to memories for the rest of her life."

Lillian leaned back in her chair and gazed at him sympathetically. "I don't have any answers or words of wisdom for you, Riley. Maybe the timing just isn't right for you and Savannah. Maybe if you'd met her ten years ago or two years from now." She shrugged helplessly and Riley stood.

"Thanks, Lillian, but as far as I'm concerned, the timing is right now. All I have to do is figure out a way to convince her of that." With those words, he walked out of the trailer and got into his truck.

As he headed for Cherokee Corners, he thought of Lillian's words about the timing perhaps being all wrong. He'd never believe that, not in a million years. He felt as if some strange sort of serendipity had been at work from the moment he'd first met Savannah.

He'd come looking to see if the crime that had taken place in the James home was like the one that had taken place in his parents' home. He could have made initial contact with the newlywed Breanna or with Clay. But fate had led him to Savannah, a woman as needy as he had been.

It had to mean something. The timing had felt intrinsically right when they'd been making love. He'd looked deep into her eyes as he'd taken possession of her, and what he'd seen shining from the brown depths of her eyes had been love...love for him.

He knew there was turmoil in her life, that the recent murders and what had happened to her parents had created havoc. But he needed to make her see that he could be her shelter in the storm, her rock to cling to. He had to convince her that he was what she needed in her life.

The problem was he couldn't find her. When he got to Cherokee Corners, he drove by her apartment first to see if her car was there. It wasn't. Then he drove to the police station, past her parents' place and by the hospital parking lot. Her car was nowhere to be found.

There was only one other place he knew to look for her, and the thought that she might be there chilled his blood.

He drove to the old bridge where her husband had plunged off the side to his death, where she'd confessed to him she sometimes climbed up in the girders and stared down at the water below.

There was only one area where a car could be

parked and a person could get to the girders to climb up, and it was to that spot that he went. Relief flooded through him as he saw that her car was nowhere in sight.

Unsure where to go next, he found himself pulling in front of the Redbud Bed and Breakfast. Maybe Alyssa, her cousin, would know where he could find her.

It was early enough in the afternoon that apparently the lunch group had gone and the after-dinner crowd hadn't yet started in. The place was empty except for Alyssa, who sat behind the counter sipping a cup of coffee.

She began to stand as he came through the door, but he waved her back down and slid onto a stool opposite her. "Hello, Mr. Frazier," she greeted him.

"Please…make it Riley."

"What can I get for you? A double-dipper cone? A hot-fudge sundae? Banana split?"

"No, no thanks. I was just wondering if maybe you knew where Savannah might be? I've been looking for her this afternoon."

"I heard from her earlier this morning, and she said she was heading into Tulsa to follow up on a tip in the McClane murder. She said that she didn't expect to be back home until late tonight."

Riley couldn't hide his disappointment. He'd hoped to talk to her now…this minute. The love he felt for her burned in his heart, in his soul and he felt the need to tell her before another hour passed, before another day went by.

"I guess you knew her husband, Jimmy," he finally said.

Alyssa nodded, her gaze holding his with a disquieting intensity. "I knew Jimmy all my life," she said. "He was a nice boy who grew into a nice man, rather quiet and utterly devoted to Savannah."

She broke eye contact with him and gazed down at the counter. "I don't know if Savannah mentioned it to you, but I have visions." She looked at him again, as if to gauge his reaction.

"Visions? You mean like psychic stuff?"

Her nod was almost imperceptive. "I've had them since I was a young child."

"So, you can see the future?" Riley was open-minded enough not to discount the possibility. After all, it was the era of people talking to the dead and psychics solving crimes for police departments. He'd never personally been touched by anything remotely paranormal, but that didn't mean he didn't believe it was possible.

She shrugged. "I see visions and sometimes they are of the future, and sometimes they are from the past. Sometimes they're about people I've never met and sometimes they're about people I love."

"And have you seen visions about Savannah?" A new tension filled Riley.

She frowned thoughtfully. "I don't have to see visions about her to know what's going on with her. When Jimmy died, something inside her died. We Cherokee believe that when people die their souls becomes spirits who walk among us." She worried a hand through her long hair, her frown deepening. "I think Savannah walks too close to Jimmy's spirit."

"I love her." The words fell from his lips before he realized he intended to say them aloud.

Alyssa smiled. "I know."

He looked at her in surprise. "You saw a vision or something?"

She laughed. "You wear your feelings for my cousin on your face, in your eyes. I don't need a vision to tell me how you feel about her." Her laughter faded and she eyed him sympathetically. "I don't know what to tell you, Riley. Savannah has been closed off from life…from love for a long time. I don't know if anyone is capable of opening her heart again."

Riley stood from his stool and raked a hand through his hair. "Wish me luck, because I intend to try."

He left the Redbud Bed and Breakfast and headed home, knowing there was nothing he could do that night. He didn't intend to give up. There was always tomorrow…or the day after…or the day after that, but sooner or later, he intended to be the man to open Savannah's heart to life…to love once again.

The week had seemed interminably long. The trip to Tulsa the day before had exhausted her, and so far the morning had been no less tiring.

Savannah drove fast toward her parents' house, hoping to arrive before Breanna and Adam brought Thomas home. She suspected Uncle Sammy wasn't the neatest of housekeepers and wanted to make sure the place was in good shape before her dad arrived home.

It was going to be difficult enough for Thomas to come home to a house where his wife wasn't there. Seventeen days. It had been seventeen long days since Rita Birdsong James had disappeared.

Although Thomas had made great strides physically since awakening from his coma, his mental state was precarious. She now arrived at the ranch and parked behind her uncle's car, then raced to the door and knocked.

Her uncle Sammy opened the door and pulled her into a bear hug. "Hi, sweetheart." He released her and stepped back to allow her in. "I heard your dad was being released, so I've been doing a little cleanup." He grinned at her, his features still retaining a boyish charm. "I'll bet you came over to make sure the place wasn't a pigsty."

She smiled ruefully. "It did cross my mind that you might need a little housekeeping help." She followed him into the kitchen, which was spotlessly clean.

"Nah, I got myself to work, decided the last thing my brother needs is to come home to a dirty place. It's bad enough he's coming home without Rita."

As always her mother's name evoked both grief and fear inside Savannah. Where was she? What was happening to her? Seventeen days felt like an eternity.

"I'm glad you're here, Uncle Sammy," she said, refusing to dwell on her mother. Right now she had enough on her mind worrying about her father. "It's nice to know you're here for Dad."

He sank down at the kitchen table and gestured for her to do the same. "I'm glad to be here. It was time for me to change my circumstances. To be honest, I was in a bit of a money crunch and was about to get kicked out of my apartment, anyway. Besides," he flashed her a wide grin, "I've always said that Cherokee Corners has the best-looking women in the world."

"Uncle Sammy, you're incorrigible," Savannah said with a laugh. At that moment they heard a car door slam out front.

Savannah and her uncle went to the door to see Breanna and Adam helping Thomas out of the car. Savannah ran outside to see if she could help.

Breanna and Adam looked incredibly stressed, which meant her father was probably in one of his moods. In the past week he'd alternated between deep depression and rage. The doctor had told them this was to be expected, but it didn't make it any easier to deal with.

"Daddy," Savannah said and hugged him tight as he got out of the passenger seat, using a cane for support. "How are you doing?"

"How do you think I'm doing?" he replied angrily. "This isn't right. This just isn't right. I shouldn't be here without her." He waved Savannah away from him with the cane as she attempted to help him toward the house. "I can walk fine on my own. I don't need any damned help."

Breanna shot Savannah a helpless look. Together Adam, Breanna and Savannah followed Thomas as he slowly made his way toward the house where Uncle Sammy stood at the front door watching their progress.

When Thomas got to the door, he grunted a hello to his brother, then went on into the living room. He stood and stared around. "My chair is gone."

"Daddy, the police took the chair. They were looking for evidence."

Tears welled up in Thomas's eyes, and the anger that had carried him inside seemed to leave him. He slumped down on the sofa. "She should be here. Where is she? What are you all doing to find her?"

"Daddy, we're doing everything we can," Savannah said. She sat next to him and placed her hand on his knee. Breanna sat on the other side of him.

"Clay is busy analyzing trace evidence, and we're following leads as fast as they develop," Breanna said. "But there just aren't that many leads to follow."

"Everyone is doing everything they can, Thomas," Uncle Sammy said.

"You have to be strong, Daddy," Savannah continued. "You have to stay strong for when she comes home. She's going to need all of us."

"She will come home, won't she?" He looked from one daughter to the other. "She'll come home and we'll all be a family again. She has to...she absolutely has to."

Savannah nodded, and the three of them hugged

as Savannah prayed that what he'd said would come true.

She went from her parents' home back to work, still chasing leads on the two murder investigations that remained unsolved and without any real viable suspects.

It was after seven when she walked into her apartment and was greeted by a meow from Happy who was apparently hungry for a little quality time.

She scooped the furry bundle up in her arms and sank down on the sofa. It was impossible to hold Happy and not think about the man who had given her to Savannah.

For the past week it had been impossible to draw a breath and not think about Riley. The feel of his skin still burned into hers, the taste of his mouth lingered. But thoughts of him were more than just about their lovemaking.

As she thought of him showing her around Riley Estates, she couldn't help but remember the beautiful sparkle of his eyes as he spoke of building a community, his enthusiasm that had been infectious.

She thought of the stories he'd told her, stories intended to make her laugh and how gentle he'd been when he'd offered her emotional support.

Each night for the past week he'd called, and she'd had to fight with herself not to pick up the receiver. After all, what was the point of talking to him anymore? What was the point in seeing him again?

She had no intention of allowing herself to be

drawn in again. She'd been weak. Her heart belonged to Jimmy and nothing and nobody could ever change that.

It would be wrong to pretend otherwise. Jimmy walked with her every day in spirit and that would be enough for her for the rest of her life.

Still, it was difficult to ignore the messages left by Riley each night. He was still searching for similar crimes in the state, and each of his phone messages began with a list of the cities and towns he'd checked out.

After he'd finished with the list, he left a more personal message…asking about her, wondering why he hadn't heard from her…hoping she was doing all right. It was the final parts of his messages that ached in her heart, his attempt to connect with her on a personal level, the memory of the nights when they'd shared those right-before-sleep telephone talks.

"Come on, sweet, let's get something to eat." She carried Happy into the kitchen and sat her on the floor near her food dish, then opened the refrigerator and stared at the contents without interest.

She couldn't remember the last time she'd been grocery shopping, and the pickings the fridge offered were slim. She finally decided to make a quick omelet. As she prepared the ingredients she studiously ignored the flashing red light on her answering machine. She knew it was probably a message from Riley. In the past two days he'd left messages for her both at the station and here at home.

She didn't want to play it. She didn't even want to hear his voice, for if she did, she'd miss him and she'd think about making love with him and she'd get excited and scared and filled with emotions she didn't want to feel.

The sound of a television game show accompanied her as she ate her dinner, but beneath the television noise she was aware of the profound silence of the apartment.

It was an absence of noise that seemed to reverberate in her head, echo deep in her heart. It created an ache inside her, the ache of loneliness.

It irritated her, because before Riley she'd had her grief to keep her company, her memories of Jimmy to make noise in her head.

She'd just finished placing her plate in the dishwasher when her phone rang once again. She knew it was Riley, felt it in her bones. She stood by the answering machine and stared at it as she waited to see who would speak to leave a message.

"Savannah...are you there?"

Riley's deep, sweetly familiar voice filled the line, and she closed her eyes, fighting the urge to pick up the phone.

"I need to talk to you," he said. "It's important...I found something." There was a long moment of silence. "We really need to talk, Savannah."

She told herself the only reason she was picking up the phone was because he'd said he'd found something important. But she also knew she couldn't spend the rest of her life avoiding him.

Besides, in the time she had known him he'd been too kind, too generous to now ignore. She at least owed him something—an explanation of why she no longer wanted to see him.

She picked up the receiver. "I'm here, Riley."

"Savannah," he said her name with relief. "I was beginning to think I'd never talk to you again."

"I've been really busy. What's up?"

He hesitated a moment, as if put off by her businesslike attitude. "I found something in my search, but I'd rather not discuss it over the phone. Can I see you?"

She frowned thoughtfully. Had he really found something important or was this just a ruse to see her again? Still, she had no reason to believe that Riley would lie to her.

"I can be there in forty-five minutes," he continued. "You'll really want to see this," he added as if recognizing she might need further incentive.

"All right. Come on over," she agreed, and she was filled with a combination of anticipation and dread at the same time.

Chapter 13

Riley hadn't been kidding when he'd told her that he'd found something that was of interest to their cases. But his driving need to see her went far beyond the information he had to impart to her.

He pulled into her apartment complex, anxious to tell her what he'd discovered, but more anxious to tell her of his feelings. He felt an urgency, somehow, that if he didn't tell her of his love for her soon something terrible might happen.

He'd learned from what had happened to his parents not to take a moment of time, of life, for granted. In a single split second of the past, he'd realized that every moment was a gift and shouldn't be wasted. He didn't want to waste another minute without telling Savannah how very important she'd become to him.

When she answered the door, his heart swelled

with his love for her. Although she was dressed in a pair of jeans and a short-sleeved button-up red blouse and had a look of exhaustion on her face, he thought she'd never looked lovelier.

He'd been so hungry to see those beautiful brown eyes, watch the fleeting flicker of emotion that danced through the brown depths. He'd been starving for the scent of her, the nearness of her, but it was obvious from her body language that she was defensive and distant.

She motioned him into the kitchen and when he sat she took the seat opposite his, obviously having no intention of sitting right beside him.

"I heard you drove into Tulsa yesterday on a hot tip on your murder case. Did anything come of it?" he asked.

"Unfortunately, it was a waste of time, although I managed to confirm the rumor that Sam McClane was a ladies' man despite the fact that he'd been married for ten years. He had a mistress in Tulsa."

He noticed that she offered him no coffee, nothing to drink. Apparently, she didn't want him to linger and didn't see this as a social visit. His heart fell at the knowledge that she'd withdrawn so far from him.

"Does that help with the investigation? Knowing that he was a ladies' man and had a mistress?"

"Yes and no. We now have several women to question concerning Sam's murder, but it doesn't help in tying the two murders to the same perpetrator, and we're all pretty convinced they were killed by the same person." Her gaze had yet to meet his fully.

"So you said on the phone you had some information for me."

He refused to be disheartened by her distance. He would take care of business first, but then they were going to have a personal talk whether she liked it or not.

He reached to open the folder he'd carried in with him and handed her a sheet of paper he'd printed off an Internet site. Shoving it across the table toward her, he wondered how she could so easily pretend that nothing had happened between them, that they hadn't been as intimate as a man and a woman could be.

As she read the paper he'd handed her, she sat up straighter in the chair and her eyes widened. "Where is this from?" she asked, finally looking fully at him for the first time.

"A town called Sequoia Falls…it's just outside of Oklahoma City."

"But it's just like what happened to us," she said, a spark of excitement shining in her eyes.

"Yeah, except it took place a year before the crime against my folks. I called the detective who was in charge of the case at the time. He's retired now, but remembered the case well."

"What did he say?" She leaned forward, and he wished she were leaning forward to be closer to him instead of in eagerness to hear what he had to say to her about the case.

"He said it was the first time he recognized that women could be as vicious as men when it came to killing. Apparently the man had been hit over the head from behind with a blunt object. The blow killed him instantly. By the time his body was found, his wife was gone. Some of her clothing and toiletries were missing, and she went to the top of the suspect list.''

"What happened with the case?"

"Still open. I found it on a site called Cold Cases in Oklahoma. The woman has never been found, dead or alive. She disappeared without a trace."

"Just like your mother and mine," Savannah said softly.

She stared down at the paper in her hand once again.

"The only difference between this case and ours is that the couple apparently was having some marital problems at the time that the crime occurred, which made it easier for the police to write it up as a domestic homicide."

He'd never wanted to take anyone in his arms as much as he wanted to her at the moment. A tiny wrinkle furrowed her brow as she once again read the newspaper account of the crime that had taken place three years earlier.

When she gazed back at him, her expression was troubled. "If we're to believe that this crime is also related to yours and mine, then what is going on here? Where are these women disappearing to?"

"I wish I knew," he said soberly.

She sighed and scooted the paper across the table back to him, the wrinkle between her eyes growing more pronounced. "What if this is some kind of a serial thing? Somebody sneaks into a house, bangs the male occupant over the head, then does something with the women? But what?''

Riley didn't reply. He had nothing to say and saw that she wasn't finished yet, that the wheels of her detective mind were still whirling.

''A crime…then the passing of a year and another crime…then the passing of two years and another. Exact same crime scene and three missing women.'' She sighed once again. ''I don't know, maybe I have serial killers on the brain and there's nothing except a strange coincidence where these three crimes are concerned.''

''Do you really believe that?''

She offered him a small smile. ''No.'' Her smile fell. ''I think it's something far more sinister than mere coincidence. Tomorrow I'll see if I can get all the official records of this particular case and see where that leads. There has to be some sort of connection…something we're missing.''

''Clay told you about the pebbles he found in my parents' house and at yours?''

She nodded. ''It's not a lot to go on, but we're checking out the quarries in the area, seeing if we can find who sells and who buys that kind of decorative rock.'' She pushed back, away from the table and he sensed a dismissal coming.

''Thanks, Riley, for bringing by the information. Who knows, maybe it will lead to something substantial.'' She stood and eyed him expectantly, but he remained seated.

"We need to talk, Savannah," he said.

He saw the flash of knowledge in her eyes, somehow knew that she'd been expecting this. She stared at the wall just over his left shoulder.

"Riley, I'm tired. It's been a long day. I appreciate you coming by to tell me what you found, but I really need to call it a night." She backed away from the table, until she bumped into the countertop across the room.

He stood. "We need to talk now, tonight because I have a feeling that if I walk out your door now we're never going to have the discussion we need to have."

She raised her chin and stared at him, resolve in her eyes. "What do you want to talk about, Riley? You want to talk about the fact that we had sex? Okay...we had sex. It's over and done and that's that."

"That's that?" He stared at her incredulously. "That's that?" In three quick strides he stood before her, so close he could smell the scent of her, see the dread that darkened her eyes. He placed his hands on her shoulders, felt the tension that made them rigid as steel.

"Honey, we did more than have sex. We made love. Having sex is what I've done throughout my adulthood. I've only made love twice...and both times were with you."

He didn't know how it was possible for eyes as dark as hers to grow even more dark, but they did. "Riley...please...I don't want to do this." She twisted from his grasp and went into the living room.

He followed behind her, but stood his ground in the center of the room, refusing to go another step toward the front door. Here he was surrounded by the photos of Jimmy…the man who held her heart captive and refused to let go.

"You don't want to do what?" he asked. "You don't want to hear that I love you? Well, you're going to hear it anyway. I love you, Savannah Tallfeather."

She winced, her eyes nearly black with pain, and she waved a hand as if to still the words that had ached for too long inside him.

He sat on the sofa and raked a hand through his hair in frustration. Somehow, some way, in his dreams, he'd thought that by confessing to her that he loved her, she'd fall into his arms and admit her love for him. He'd thought hearing the words spoken aloud would make it real for her, right for her.

But the look on her face was anything but love…it was horror and fear and a touch of anger. "Savannah," he said softly. "The one thing my mother and father wanted for me more than anything else on this earth was love. Oh, they wanted me to be successful, financially stable and all that, but more than anything they wanted me to find a woman to share my life. I found her in you, Savannah."

"No…no you haven't," she exclaimed, her eyes liquid as if she were fighting back tears. "We've been thrown together because of the crimes that wrecked our lives. That's all it is, Riley."

"That's not all it is," he protested. He got up, feeling at a distinct disadvantage sitting while she stood halfway across the room. He took a step toward her. There was a knot in his chest as he gazed at her. "I love you, Savannah. Marry me and share my life."

This was the conversation she'd hoped to avoid. Only it was worse than she'd anticipated. She hadn't expected a confession of love...a proposal of marriage.

She hated him at that moment, hated him because there was a part of her that wanted to throw herself into his arms, there was a part of her that longed to agree to share his life, his future.

There was a part of her that wanted to forsake Jimmy, and she knew it was a wicked, selfish part of her. And she didn't know if she hated him or hated herself.

"No, Riley. I can't marry you."

He approached where she stood, and what she wanted more than anything was to run away, to disappear. She didn't want him close enough to touch her, didn't want him near enough so she could smell the wonderfully male scent of him. She didn't want him to weaken her resolve.

"Why not? Why won't you marry me?" He stopped only when he stood close enough to her that she felt his breath warm her face, his body heat radiate through her.

She wanted to melt into him, seek the warmth and shelter of his arms, and that sickened her, for what kind of woman did that make her?

"Savannah," his voice was a soft plea filled with

emotion that tugged at her heart. He reached out and took one of her hands in his. She tried to pull away, but he held tight, refusing to grant her the distance she so desperately needed.

"I know you feel as if your life is in turmoil right now. I know you have the murders on your mind, and the pain of your mother's absence. But let me be your sanity. Hang on to me when things get crazy…let my love for you sustain you."

His eyes, those beautiful blue eyes of his were filled with such longing, with a depth of love she'd only seen in one other man's eyes before. Jimmy's eyes.

With a sharp pull, she yanked her hand from his grasp. "Don't make this hard for me, Riley." She took a step backward, tears momentarily obscuring her vision. "I've had my love, Riley. His name was Jimmy Tallfeather, and he was my soul mate. I gave my heart to him and now there's nothing left for me to give to anyone else."

His gaze remained soft and tender as it lingered on her. "I'm not asking you to forget Jimmy and the love the two of you shared. I would never try to take that away from you. But surely there's room in your heart for me, too."

Room in her heart? She had a whole houseful of him in her heart. But it wasn't real. It couldn't be real. It was love based on sheer emotion, on raging hormones and the commonality of their situations.

She couldn't look at him, was afraid that if she

gazed into his eyes once again she'd be lost. "I'm sorry, Riley," she said, staring down at her feet.

She gasped as he grabbed her by the shoulders. "Look at me, Savannah. Look at me and tell me that you don't love me."

"I don't," she said as tears splashed down on her cheeks. Still she refused to look at him.

"I don't believe you. You can lie to me with your mouth, but you can't lie to me with your eyes, and when you look at me, I see love there. You can't lie to me with your kisses, because when I kiss you I taste love. And you can't lie with your heartbeat, and when I felt it racing with mine as we made love, I felt your love."

"It doesn't matter," she said, twisting away from him. "It doesn't matter what I feel for you or what you feel for me. I had my chance at happiness. I married my soul mate. He walks with me in spirit every day. I've already dishonored his memory enough by making love with you."

For the first time since he'd arrived she saw a flash of something in his eyes—a kindling of a fire that had nothing to do with love or desire. "What do you think? There's a quota on soul mates and you've met yours so you don't get another one?"

He reached out as if to grab her once again, but she sidestepped him, feeling as if she'd shatter into a million pieces if he touched her one more time. "Savannah, the moment I met you, the moment I got a chance to talk to you, I felt a connection like I'd never felt before. And every moment I've spent with you has only confirmed to me that we're soul mates. We were destined to meet, to share our lives together. I want to marry you. I want you to have my children, to share my dreams.''

Each of his words was like a knife through her heart. A torturous emotional conflict raged inside her. On the one hand she yearned to fall into his arms, to take a chance on what he offered.

But she didn't have to take a chance on Jimmy's love. It had been a constant presence in her life since she'd been a young girl. Jimmy would love her forever and always.

Jimmy had adored her. He'd spent his life with her happiness as his only real goal. Didn't she owe him more? Didn't she owe him a heart full of memories, a heart so filled with him that there was no room for any other man?

She looked at the array of photographs on the end table next to the sofa, her gaze locking on her favorite, the one of Jimmy in his parka.

''He's gone, Savannah.'' Before she realized he'd moved, Riley was in front of her. He once again grabbed her by the shoulders and forced her to look into his eyes.

''Jimmy is gone and he's never coming back.'' Riley's eyes burned into hers with fierce intensity. ''He's your past, Savannah. Let it go…let him go and let me be your future.''

She wasn't sure why, but anger coursed through her at his words, a rich anger that half blinded her. How dare he tell her to forget the man who had been the love of her life. How dare he tell her to let go of the man she had pledged her love, her life to.

She jerked away from him. "You're one to talk about letting go of the past, Riley. You've kept your parents' house like a shrine, waiting for people to just walk back in after a two-year absence."

He reeled backward as if she'd physically struck him, and shame washed over her. She hadn't meant what she'd said, but he'd made her so angry. "Riley…I'm sorry, that wasn't fair." She could barely see him through her tears, and this time it was she who took a step toward him.

He held up a hand to stop her, his jaw clenched tight. "No, you're right. But there's a difference between me clinging to the past and you clinging to the past." He reached out and grabbed her favorite photo of Jimmy off the table.

"The difference is my mother's body has never been found. I never got the luxury of a funeral, of saying goodbye. Your husband's body was found. He's buried in the Cherokee Corners Cemetery." His voice was hard and she knew she'd made him angry. "I don't know if my mother is ever coming back. But you know Jimmy never is. That's the difference."

"Riley…I'm sorry," she repeated.

"Is this what you want for your future?" He held the photo out before him. "A photograph to keep you warm at night, memories for companionship? You love me, Savannah. I know you do, but you're a coward. You'd rather hold on tight to a dead man than face the possibilities with me. You're afraid to take a chance on loving again...on living again.''

He reached out to place the photo back on the table, but somehow the photo slipped off the edge and, as if in slow motion, it fell to the floor where the glass shattered into a hundred pieces.

He looked at her, obviously horrified. ''Savannah...''

''Just go, Riley,'' she exclaimed. ''Just get out of here. There's nothing here for you.''

For a long moment he gazed at her, and in his gaze she saw all his love for her, all the dreams he would have shared with her, all the desire that would have been hers. Then he turned away and stalked out of the house.

She stood like a statue, tears coursing down her cheeks as she played and replayed their conversation in her mind. He loved her. He wanted to build a life with her. He'd wanted her to have his children.

Children. She and Jimmy had talked about having babies, but the time had never seemed right. She'd thought her desire for babies had died with Jimmy, but the moment Riley had mentioned her having his babies a well of want had opened inside her.

On leaden legs she moved to where the picture had crashed, and bent down to pick up the pieces of glass. Thankfully the photo wasn't damaged, but the frame had been destroyed.

He wouldn't be back, she thought as she swept the last of the glass into a dustpan. There would be no more evening phone calls, no more messages left on her machine. She would no longer enjoy his smile, his laughter, his kisses. He was gone and she knew in her heart he wouldn't be back.

She plucked the photo of Jimmy from the damaged frame and held it to her. This was her past…and this was her future. What she didn't know was if the sobs that now choked her were for Jimmy…or Riley…or for herself.

As Savannah wept, her mother explored the room where she was held captive, fighting the fear that had taken hold of her ever since total consciousness had claimed her.

She'd begun to keep track of time by when the slot in the door would open and a tray of food would be handed to her. No words were ever spoken despite her pleading, begging for the person on the other side of the door to let her go, talk to her, explain why she was here.

In the mornings she got a cheese omelet, toast and coffee. Noontime brought a chicken or turkey sandwich, a small salad and a soda…what she often ate for lunch at home. Dinner was usually a broiled chicken breast, some kind of vegetables and the bean bread that was traditionally Cherokee and one of her favorite foods.

She wondered if it was a fellow Cherokee who held her? She was clear enough in the mind to recognize it wasn't a mythical Raven Mocker holding her. But if it was another of her people, then why?

She'd marked four days since she'd become conscious of time and had no idea how many days before that she'd been here. What was she being held for?

When she wasn't exploring the room, trying to find some way out or at least to summon help, she thought of her family. She tried not to think of Thomas, for the pain of thinking of him was too great to bear.

Instead she focused on her children. She worried about Clay, knew that her absence would be deeply felt by him because they'd had a tiff right before she'd been kidnapped.

It all seemed so silly now. She'd wanted him to take part in one of the ceremonies at the Cherokee Cultural Center, but as usual he'd refused.

Her son had always been somewhat of an enigma to her. Something had happened to him when he'd been a teenager that had made him turn his back on his Cherokee heritage. She'd watched him transform from a carefree, loving young man into an angry loner who seemed to find pleasure only in his work.

Thankfully, after Breanna had been left by the man who had married her, gotten her pregnant, then left her, she'd finally found love with Adam. With the kind, strong Adam by her side, Rita knew Breanna would be fine.

Savannah was another worry. When she'd lost her husband, Jimmy, a little over a year before, she'd lost not only the sparkle in her eyes, the smile on her lips, but her interest in living, as well. Oh, she went through the motions, going to work, visiting with her siblings, but there was a darkness in her heart, a barrier around her that Rita and nobody else seemed able to penetrate.

"Keep them safe," Rita whispered aloud. "And, please, make me strong enough to survive whatever lies ahead."

Chapter 14

It had been two days since he'd left Savannah's apartment, and still the ache in Riley's heart hadn't eased one little bit.

He alternated between being incredibly angry with her and wanting to rush back over to her place and try again. But pride kept him from going over or calling her. She'd told him there was nothing for him there, had never said that she loved him, and he'd be a fool to pursue it any further.

She was bound to her dead husband, and there was apparently nothing that would break that bond. Riley had given her all that he had to give, but it hadn't been enough. Jimmy Tallfeather must have been one hell of a man.

He reared back in his chair and looked out the window, where storm clouds threatened. All day long dark turbulent clouds had chased each other across the sky, promising that before the day was done there would be a storm.

So far they'd been lucky, and the rain had held off for the workday. That was important because they'd begun digging a new lot to prepare it for the foundation work. If they were really lucky, the dark clouds would blow over completely without shedding a drop of rain and therefore not stopping the work on the job site.

Business was booming, but Riley hadn't felt any kind of excitement about it since the day he'd brought Savannah to Riley Estates. On that day he'd dreamed of sharing all this with her. He would never suggest she quit her job as a cop, but he saw visions of evenings together with her sharing the events of her days and him sharing his.

He'd envisioned her helping him plan new ways to serve families in the community he was creating, had dreamed of going to sleep each night with her in his arms after making love to her.

Dreams and fantasies, wishes and hopes, that's all they had been. But, damn it, he'd wanted them to be real. He'd wanted it all with her.

Irritated by his continuous thoughts of Savannah, he got up out of his chair and went to the window, where he could see a cloud of dust rising from the earthwork being done on a distant lot.

She'd been right about one thing: he had been clinging to the past where his parents' place was concerned. He'd fooled himself into believing that after all this time, one day his mother would just reappear and pick up the life that had been left behind.

It was time to stop fooling himself. Even if she did come back, she wouldn't be the same woman she had once been. Whatever she'd been through, whatever had happened would have transformed her forever.

The house he'd kept exactly as it had been when she'd been there was nothing more than an empty shell filled with items that had served their life span. For him, it was time to let go.

With this decision in mind, he picked up the phone and dialed the number of a friend in real estate sales who had also been a friend of his parents. "Janet," he greeted her as she answered her phone. "It's Riley."

"Don't tell me...you've finally broken down and decided I can handle your homes in the Riley Estates."

He laughed. She'd been at him since the first home had gone up, wanting an exclusive to sell his homes. "Not a chance. Why should I split my hard-earned money with you?"

"I keep telling you, honey, you let the buyers pay my commission."

"Not interested," Riley replied.

"All right, I won't push anymore." She released a long, practiced sigh. "So, what's up? What can I do for you?"

For a moment the words stuck in his throat. Letting go was easy in thought, more difficult in actuality. It

was a little bit frightening, and more than a little
bit sad.

"Riley? You still there?" Janet asked.

"I'm here." He drew a deep breath. "I was wondering if you'd handle the sale of my parents' house."

There was a long moment of silence, then she finally spoke. "Honey, are you sure?"

"Don't you think it's time?" he countered.

"It's past time," she said softly. "I loved her, too,
Riley, but it's been a long time. It serves no purpose
for that house to stay like it has been."

"It will take me a couple of weeks to pack things
up and get them into storage someplace."

"Take whatever time you need. Call me when
you're ready, and we'll sit down and figure out a selling price."

"Thanks, Janet. I appreciate it."

"No problem, and Riley…it's the right thing to
do."

He hung up and once again left his chair and
moved back to the window, feeling an odd sense of
relief now that he'd made the decision to let go. If
his mother, by some miracle, ever returned, she knew
where Riley lived. She'd know how to find him.

Now, if there was just a way he could wave a wand
and help Savannah to let go. But he couldn't. He
didn't have a magic wand in his possession.

Maybe she just didn't love him enough. Maybe it
would be another man who would reawaken her to
life, to love. Maybe eventually she'd find a man who
would convince her to put her deceased husband in

the past and face a new future. He just couldn't imagine that man not being him.

He frowned as he saw his foreman's truck roaring toward the trailer. There was still an hour of work time left. This could only be trouble. If the foreman was threatening for the sixth time to quit, Riley would let him. He was tired of the old man's temperament.

Leslie Heaton, the burly older man who'd been in the construction business for years, climbed out of his truck and moved faster than Riley had ever seen him toward the trailer. Riley instantly went on alert.

"Boss." Leslie yelled the moment he entered the trailer.

"What's wrong?" Riley faced the foreman, whose usual ruddy complexion was pale as a summer night moon.

"We'd just started 'dozing on lot fifty-four and we turned up something." If it was possible, Leslie's face grew more pale. "We need to call the cops. There's a body out there, boss."

Riley made the call to the Cherokee Corners Police Department, then stood on the front porch of the trailer to wait for their arrival. In the calm before the storm he knew was about to occur, he tried to keep his mind blank.

He had no idea if the body found was that of a man or a woman, had no reason to believe that it had anything at all to do with him personally. But there was a ball of dread in his stomach that only grew bigger as streaks of lightning flashed across the sky followed by an explosive clap of thunder.

"All I know for certain is that Sam McClane was a ladies' man and Greg Maxwell apparently had a good and stable marriage. Sam's wife has a solid alibi for the night of his murder. She was at a fund-raiser for our mayor at the time of his murder." Savannah slumped into the chair opposite Glen Cleberg's desk as she finished giving what little report she had on the murders.

"This isn't good enough, Savannah. We've got to get these solved. It's the mayor who's busting my butt about the fact that we have two heinous unsolved murders in a town where murder has been rare."

"I know, I know, but what do you want me to do, Glen?" she said irritably.

"I want you to solve these cases."

"Yeah, well I wouldn't mind doing the same," she snapped. She ruffled a hand through her hair and drew a deep breath to calm herself. She'd felt as if every nerve in her body was on edge since her last encounter with Riley.

"No witnesses have come forward. I've chased down every lead that has come in. I'm still waiting for some of the forensic reports to come back, but I can only do what I can do."

"Well, try to do better," Glen said, and she knew these final words were a dismissal.

She left his office and flung herself into her desk

chair, fighting against anger and frustration, depression and grief.

The things Riley had said to her when he'd left the other night had been playing in her head, causing her near sleepless nights. When she did sleep she dreamed of Riley and Jimmy, and in the dreams Jimmy was nearly transparent and when he tried to wrap his arms around her all she felt was chilled and empty.

Was it time to give up her grief? The thought was so frightening. Her grief had become a warm and familiar friend and to live without it meant opening herself up to other human emotions.

"Heard you got your butt chewed by the chief."

She looked up to see Jason Sheller standing in front of her desk, his usual smirk crossing his handsome face. "Somebody must have exaggerated, my butt is just fine, thank you very much."

He raised a dark eyebrow. "That's the understatement of the day. Your butt is more than fine."

"Go away, Jason," she exclaimed.

Instead, he sat in the chair opposite her desk. "I was just wondering what kind of progress you're making on the murders? Got any suspects?" He wiggled in the chair, his gaze not quite meeting hers.

"Why do you care? You don't work homicide."

"Just curious, that's all. So, got any suspects?"

Savannah sighed, realizing the best way to get rid of him was to give him what he wanted. "Initially, Greg Maxwell's wife was at the top of my suspect list in his murder, then Sam McClane wound up dead.

I can't tie her to Sam and we're pretty sure the same perp killed both men, so Virginia is off the list for now and nobody else has taken her place."

"Bummer," he said. "Sounds like you've hit a dead end." To her relief he got up. "Keep me posted, would you? Maxwell was a friend of mine." He wandered back toward the break room, and Savannah sighed once again.

Odd, she hadn't known that Jason even knew the Maxwells. She sighed. Murder cases, a missing mother, a grieving, angry father…and Riley. She felt as if her head might explode from all the chaos inside.

Thomas's transition from the hospital to the house had not been a smooth one. Twice today Uncle Sammy had called her to tell her that Thomas was out of control, throwing things and cursing, then weeping inconsolably.

Savannah had told him to call the doctor and see if there was anything he could do. But she knew there was nothing anyone could do other than find her mother safe and sound and return her to the man who loved her with all his heart. Nothing would be right in Thomas's life until the day Rita was returned to him.

And nothing would be right in her life ever. Riley had been her single chance for moving on, but he'd been right. She was a coward, afraid to face an uncertain future with him when she could cling to the memory and the thought of what might have been with Jimmy.

"You're my woman, Silver Star," Jimmy had said

to her so often. "You're my woman forever and always." But neither of them had known that forever and always would only last two years.

The phone rang, and for a moment she hesitated to pick it up. What if it was Riley? She quickly dismissed the very idea. He hadn't called since the night he'd left, and the absence of his nightly phone calls had only increased her sense of loneliness, of emptiness in what she called her life.

She grabbed up the phone. "Officer Tallfeather."

"Savannah, it's me."

"Hi, Bree." She relaxed a bit as she heard her sister's familiar voice. "How's my favorite sister?"

Breanna laughed, sounding oddly happy. "I believe I'm your only sister."

"Then, how is my favorite niece?"

"A handful," Breanna replied, but Savannah could hear the smile in her sister's voice. "She's particularly excited today."

"Why? What's going on today?"

"She's just learned she's going to be a big sister."

It took a moment for Breanna's words to sink in, then Savannah gasped in surprise. "Oh, Bree! You're pregnant?"

"I am." She laughed with happiness. "You're the first person I've told…I mean beside Adam and Maggie. I figured this family needed a little good news."

"That's great news. I'm so happy for you. Tell Maggie I know she's going to be a terrific big sister."

"I will. I've got to run now. Even though I'm only

eight weeks along, Adam seems to think we need to go out today and buy a few things.''

"Go and have fun. We'll talk later.'' The two sisters hung up.

Savannah was thrilled for Bree. She'd been so lucky in meeting Adam, who had moved into the little rental house next to her Victorian home. Love had bloomed, marriage had followed and now a baby was on the way.

Yes, Savannah was positively thrilled for her sister but she couldn't seem to control the tears that seeped from her eyes and ran down her cheeks.

Lucky, lucky Breanna. Her house would be filled with children and love and laughter. There would be no children for Savannah. No laughter, no love would fill her small apartment.

"Hey, have you heard?'' Jason came toward her desk, a cup of coffee in his hand.

"Heard what?''

"You know that guy you've been seeing…that builder from Sycamore Ridge?''

"Riley Frazier. What about him?'' Even his name on her lips made a pain shoot through her. She stood and grabbed her purse, deciding she was ready to call it a day.

"I just heard from one of the guys in the break room that apparently they were digging a foundation out at his place and found a body.''

"A body?'' Horror swept through her and it was suddenly difficult to draw a breath.

"Yeah, guess his business will be shut down for a

few days. But the real stinker of it is, the body has been identified as his mother.'' He jumped back in surprise as she shoved past him.

Blindly she pushed past him and headed for the station house door. Pain like she'd never known before raked through her.

Riley. Poor Riley. His mother was dead. She was dead...dead. The words reverberated around and around in her head as she ran for her car.

She had to get out of here...she had to go.

The hope she'd entertained that her own mother would be found alive and well crashed and burned with the news that Riley's mother was dead...had probably been dead since the day she'd gone missing.

But Savannah's pain went beyond that knowledge. Her pain was too enormous to figure out its source, it was a combination of shattered hopes and broken lives and unfulfilled dreams. It was the stark, raving pain of the living.

She got into her car and began to drive, not knowing, not caring where she was going, just knowing the need to try to outrun her pain.

A nightmare. Riley felt as if he'd been plunged back into his deepest, darkest nightmare. He'd thought he'd prepared himself for the knowledge that his mother was probably dead, but he knew now there was no way to prepare oneself for such a thing.

It hadn't taken long to make the identification. Joanna Frazier still wore the distinctive wedding ring her husband had bought for her so many years before.

Around her neck was a locket, with a picture of Riley inside.

The police had brought him the ring and locket and in the first instant of seeing the two pieces of jewelry, that last vestige of hope he'd maintained had shattered. He'd clutched the last of his hope in his hand and had known the pain of deep bereavement.

Both his parents were gone now. He was alone…utterly alone in the world. From that moment the evening had been a study in sheer torture.

Yellow crime-scene tape took on a garish aura as the ominous clouds overhead grew darker. Workers stood in small groups, waiting for the police to talk to them.

Riley had already been grilled for several hours as the murder of his father was revisited and new questions were asked about his mother.

The County Medical Examiner had already left after determining that his mother had been killed by blunt-force trauma to her head.

The bulldozer operator had indicated that the body had been uncovered with the first scraping of earth. It had been a relatively shallow grave.

"At least you finally know," Lillian had told him when the news had come that it was his mother they had found. "At least you finally have some closure." She'd hugged him tight, and he'd welcomed the warmth of her hug.

Yes, he now had closure. For that he was grateful. The unknowing had always been difficult, and deep in his heart, in a place he'd never really wanted to acknowledge, he'd always known she was probably gone.

He waited until the last of his workers had been dismissed, and only then did he leave the trailer and head for home.

It was while he was driving home that his thoughts turned to Savannah. A sudden fear gripped him. Had she heard? Did she know that his mother had been found dead?

He'd known for some time that somehow in her mind she'd tied the two women together—his mother and hers, both missing, but hope not lost.

If she'd heard that his mother had been found dead, then what state of mind would she be in? No matter what had happened between the two of them, no matter that she couldn't love him enough to have any kind of future with him. He loved her enough to be scared.

She hadn't promised him. When he'd asked her to promise that she'd never again go to the bridge, never again allow the pain of life to drive her over the edge, she'd refused to promise him that.

He had to find her. He had to make certain she was all right. He wasn't sure why, but as he headed toward Cherokee Corners, a terrible sense of dread accompanied him.

Chapter 15

He drove fast despite the slash of lightning that rent the blackened sky and the crashes of thunder that shook his car.

He, more than anyone, knew how fragile Savannah was and he feared that the news about his mother's death would drive her straight over the edge. He didn't fear for her sanity. He feared for her very life.

She wouldn't promise me. She refused to promise me. Over and over again these words played and replayed in his head, haunting him, scaring him.

Deep in his heart he knew that the driving need to see that she was okay was compounded by his own need to hold her, to help ease the pain he felt at knowing his mother was truly and really gone.

By some miracle the rain continued to hold off. It

was as if the heavens knew that enough tears would be shed tonight so the clouds' weeping wasn't necessary.

He drove by her parents' place on the way into town, but her car wasn't there. When he reached Cherokee Corners the first place he went was her apartment. But her car wasn't in its usual place in the parking lot. The next place he checked was the police station.

Despite the fact that he didn't see her vehicle, he parked and went inside. Maybe she was out chasing some lead and hadn't heard the news about his mother. He hoped that was the case. If she had to hear the news, he thought it would be better if she heard it from him.

He was greeted in the police station by a handsome officer who introduced himself as Jason Sheller. "Yeah, she was here, but she flew out of here like a bat out of hell a couple of hours ago," he informed Riley.

"Do you know where she was going?" Riley asked, a sense of urgency filling his soul.

Jason shook his head. "Don't have a clue. But, hey, sorry to hear about your mother."

So, the news had made the rounds here in Cherokee Corners already. "Thanks," he said distractedly. "Did Savannah know…about my mother?"

"Yeah, it was the last thing I told her before she flew out of here." Jason offered him a sly grin. "I figured she was on her way to console you. I know you two have a thing going on."

The words irritated Riley, seeming to diminish

what he felt for Savannah. "That *thing* is called love and I need to find her."

"Can't help you there," Jason said with a shrug.

Riley didn't waste any more time. He left the police station knowing there was one other place she could possibly be, and the thought of her there chilled him to the bone.

The storm outside seemed to have intensified, the sky electric and noisy as Riley got back into his car. Fear slashed through him as lightning lacerated the black night.

If she had lost all hope of finding her mother alive, had she also lost the last of her will to live? Was she finally ready to make that leap into the river to join her husband in the spirit world?

"No." The single word ripped from his throat.

His heart pounded as loudly in his ears as the thunder boomed overhead. Even if Savannah didn't love him, he didn't want her to join her Jimmy.

He wanted her alive and well and even if it wasn't with him, he wanted her to find love and happiness once again with another man.

He didn't want the authorities dragging the river for her body. He stepped on the gas, frantic, as sweat beaded up on his forehead. He had to get to that bridge and he hoped, he prayed she wasn't there... that it wasn't too late.

His heart tumbled to the depths of hell as he approached the bridge and saw her car parked nearby. "God...no," he whispered as he parked his car and plunged out.

He stared up at the structure, but found it impossible to see clearly in the darkness. He got back into his car and reached into the glove box for a flashlight.

''Please God,'' he prayed as he once again left the car. The grass and underbrush between the road and the base of the bridge was overgrown, thick with tangles and thorny bushes. He clicked on the flashlight to aid him as he made his way to the old wooden structure.

As he hurried through the brush, he alternated between shining the light on the ground just ahead of him and upward toward the bridge, but the light wasn't strong enough to allow him to see anything, anyone that the bridge support might harbor.

When a flash of lightning occurred, he quickly looked upward, but before he could focus, the light was gone, replaced by a thunderous roar that sounded like God's fury.

He had no capacity for any thought except for her. Savannah filled his every pore, she raced in his heart. The need to save her from herself usurped any other desire, superceded anything he'd ever wanted in his life.

He reached the bottom of the bridge and once again shone the light upward. ''Savannah!'' Her name ripped from his throat, but was swallowed by a booming clap of thunder.

''Savannah!'' he yelled again, the anguished cry coming from the very depths of him.

He focused his light first on one area of the bridge, then on another, and a sob escaped him as he finally saw her, crouched in the underbelly of the structure, sitting on a support beam just over the river below.

Looking around frantically, he saw the way he suspected she'd climbed up, a crisscross of beams that created a kind of ladder.

Laying the flashlight on the ground with the beam pointed in that direction, he grabbed the first beam and began to ascend.

"Savannah," he yelled once again as he got closer. In the flash of lightning he saw her turn her head toward him, shock momentarily shining on her features.

"Riley...get down," she said.

In another flash of light he saw that her face was shiny with tears. He didn't get down. Instead he went higher. "Not without you," he replied.

Thunder rattled the earth, and Riley clung to the wood, for a moment afraid that they'd both be shaken off into the river below.

"Please, Savannah, please come down with me. Just because my mother was found dead doesn't mean there isn't still hope for yours. Don't do this. You can't do this. Even if you don't love me, don't do this to your family, don't do this to yourself. You have people who love you, who need you in their lives."

For a moment he thought it had begun to rain, for his face was wet. Then he realized it was tears...tears for her, for her pain, for the anguish that would drive her to be here now.

"Riley, get down before you fall," she exclaimed, and he heard fear in her voice.

He held out a hand toward her even though he wasn't close enough to touch her yet. "I told you, I'm not leaving without you."

Lightning flashed once again, and their gazes met. In hers was an expression he couldn't read, but it didn't appear to be the expression of a woman on the verge of suicide.

A sob released itself from him again as she scooted toward him. Closer…closer…closer she came, then her hand was in his.

Together they descended the bridge support and it was only when they reached the firmness of the ground beneath them that he pulled her tight against his chest.

He held her so tight it was impossible for her to speak, impossible for her to do anything else but desperately cling to him.

When he finally released her, he framed her face with his hands. "There's life after tragedy, Savannah. No matter how desperate you feel right now, no matter how bleak things seem at the moment, it passes. Even if you don't love me, even if you don't want to build a life with me, at least believe me when I tell you that things will get better."

"I do believe you," she replied softly. She paused a moment as thunder roared, then continued in the stillness that followed. "Oh, Riley. I didn't go up there to jump off the bridge. I went up there to say goodbye…goodbye to the past…goodbye to Jimmy."

"Goodbye?" he echoed in surprise.

She nodded and took a step back from him. "I'm so sorry about your mother." Tears filled her eyes. "I'm so sorry for your loss. It was when I heard the news that I realized everything in my life had changed."

"What do you mean?"

Lightning flashed, and she waited for the responding blast of thunder before speaking once again. "Riley, when I heard about your mother, the only thing I wanted…I needed to do was be with you. I wanted to be the one who grieved with you, who held you if you cried. I wanted to be the one to help pick up the pieces, and I knew then how deeply, how completely I love you."

He started to move toward her, but she held up a hand to stop him. She needed to talk, to get out all the emotions that had assailed her over the past couple of hours. "At first I thought it was just the shock of finding out about your mother. My first reaction was to run here…to be with Jimmy."

She turned and looked at the river, which reflected the turbulence of the sky overhead. "I've always found a certain amount of peace here. I'd climb up there and talk to Jimmy, see his face reflected in the waters below. But this time there was no peace for me and when I looked in the water, all I saw was you."

She turned back to look at him. "I knew then that it was time to say goodbye." Her words caused pain to swell in her heart, but she knew there would always be a certain amount of pain when she thought of the man who had once been her husband.

"Jimmy was a wonderful man with a beautiful heart, but he wouldn't have wanted me to close off my heart because he was no longer here. He would have wanted me to go on, to find happiness. I'm ready, Riley. I'm ready to take that chance on you...if you'll still have me."

"Still have you?" In one long stride he had her wrapped in his arms once again. "Savannah, when I thought of this earth without you in it, my heart went dead inside. Even if I couldn't have you in my life, I needed to know that you were okay, that you'd eventually find love and happiness."

"I want that with you, Riley. I think you're right, there isn't a quota on soul mates. I've been lucky, Jimmy was my first soul mate...but you, you're my second and hopefully my last."

She could speak no more, for his mouth covered hers in a kiss that absolutely took her breath away. Filled with love and desire, the kiss confirmed what she knew in her heart. It was time to move on with this man that fate had brought her way.

At that moment, the skies opened up and rain began to pelt them. With a squeal, Savannah jumped away from him, but he grabbed her by the hand and pulled her toward his car. "Come on," he said. "I'll bring you back to your car later. I'm not letting you out of my sight for a second."

Laughing with an abandon she hadn't felt in over a year, she raced with him to his car through the pouring rain. She felt so light, so filled with possibility, with happiness.

When they reached his truck and were in the dry interior, she turned to him, realizing that her epiphany of where her happiness lay had come at a tremendous cost...the discovery of his mother's body.

"Riley, I'm so sorry about your mother."

Although his eyes darkened, he nodded. "It's all right. I've known in my heart for a long time that she wasn't coming back, that she was probably dead." He reached across and took her hand. "But you can't lose hope about your mother. According to the medical examiner, my mom had been dead for no longer than four or five months."

"Four or five months?" Savannah was grateful for the warmth of his hand around hers. "But, Riley, she'd been missing for almost two years."

"That's my point, honey. If the person who killed my father and took my mother is also responsible for what happened to your father and mother, then whoever had my mother kept her alive for over a year. You have to hang on to that fact. My mother was alive for about sixteen months after she disappeared."

He reached out and pulled her into his arms, and she came willingly, knowing that even though he'd just suffered a tremendous loss, his thought was to ease her pain.

"It doesn't make sense, does it?" she asked. "That your mother was alive for all that time and yet we don't know where she was, what she was doing."

His arm tightened around her. "No, it doesn't make

sense. But I'm certain of one thing. If she'd been able to, she would have been home. The only thing that makes sense to me is that she was being held somewhere…a prisoner.''

A chill walked up Savannah's spine as she thought of her own mother. Was that the answer? Had she been taken captive on the night Thomas had been hit over the head? It had been nineteen days since that night. How many days did they have before she was found like Riley's mother, in a shallow grave?

She shook as another chill possessed her.

''Let's get out of here,'' he said. ''We need to get you someplace dry. We'll come back tomorrow to get your car.'' He started the engine of his truck, but before he pulled away from the bridge, he turned back to look at her.

''Someway or another you'll get through all this, Savannah. I'll make sure you do. I'll be your strength.''

She shook her head. ''I don't need you to be my strength, Riley. Alyssa once told me I'm one of the strongest people she knows. At the time, I didn't believe her, but as I sat up there telling Jimmy goodbye, I realized that I am strong. But that doesn't mean I don't need you to love me.''

''I do. I love you, Savannah Tallfeather.''

''And I love you, Riley Frazier,'' she said.

Again his lips sought hers in a kiss that spoke of her future. Despite the fact that her mother was missing, that she had two unsolved murders on her plate, in spite of the fact that she would always hold sweet memories of the man she had lost to the waters of the Cherokee River, she felt a happiness that had no boundaries.

It was the happiness of a future filled with a man who would share her dreams, a man who would give her passion and love in return for her own, a man who was the builder of dreams—the man who would be her husband, her life.

"Take me home, Riley. Take me to my house. I want you in my bed."

His eyes shone bright from the truck's interior lights. "At this moment, I feel as if I'm the luckiest man on earth," he said softly. "I can't believe fate brought you to me, I can't believe that after all these years, finally fate has brought me my soul mate."

Savannah snuggled against his side as he put the truck in drive and pulled away from the bridge. Goodbye, Jimmy, she thought. There will always be a place in my heart for you and what we shared, but now there's a new place opened in my heart, a space to allow in new love, new life...Riley.

*   *   *   *   *

Don't miss the next book in
Carla Cassidy's miniseries
CHEROKEE CORNERS, *TRACE EVIDENCE,*
featuring Clay James, on sale in
December 2003.

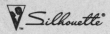

If you enjoyed what you just read,
then we've got an offer you can't resist!

Take 2 bestselling love stories FREE!

Plus get a FREE surprise gift!

Clip this page and mail it to Silhouette Reader Service™

IN U.S.A.	IN CANADA
3010 Walden Ave.	P.O. Box 609
P.O. Box 1867	Fort Erie, Ontario
Buffalo, N.Y. 14240-1867	L2A 5X3

YES! Please send me 2 free Silhouette Intimate Moments® novels and my free surprise gift. After receiving them, if I don't wish to receive anymore, I can return the shipping statement marked cancel. If I don't cancel, I will receive 6 brand-new novels every month, before they're available in stores! In the U.S.A., bill me at the bargain price of $3.99 plus 25¢ shipping and handling per book and applicable sales tax, if any*. In Canada, bill me at the bargain price of $4.74 plus 25¢ shipping and handling per book and applicable taxes**. That's the complete price and a savings of at least 10% off the cover prices—what a great deal! I understand that accepting the 2 free books and gift places me under no obligation ever to buy any books. I can always return a shipment and cancel at any time. Even if I never buy another book from Silhouette, the 2 free books and gift are mine to keep forever.

245 SDN DNUV
345 SDN DNUW

Name	(PLEASE PRINT)	
Address	Apt.#	
City	State/Prov.	Zip/Postal Code

* Terms and prices subject to change without notice. Sales tax applicable in N.Y.
** Canadian residents will be charged applicable provincial taxes and GST.
   All orders subject to approval. Offer limited to one per household and not valid to
   current Silhouette Intimate Moments® subscribers.
   ® are registered trademarks of Harlequin Books S.A., used under license.

INMOM02   ©1998 Harlequin Enterprises Limited

✂ **Your opinion is important to us!** Please take a few moments to share your
thoughts with us about your experiences with Harlequin and Silhouette books.
Your comments will be very useful in ensuring that we deliver books you love to read.
*Please take a few minutes to complete the questionnaire,
then send it to us at the address below.*

Send your completed questionnaires to:
Harlequin/Silhouette Reader Survey, P.O. Box 9046, Buffalo, NY 14269-9046

1. As you may know, there are many different lines under the Harlequin and Silhouette
brands. Each of the lines is listed below. Please check the box that most represents
your reading habit for each line.

Line	Currently read this line	Do not read this line	Not sure if I read this line
Harlequin American Romance	❏	❏	❏
Harlequin Duets	❏	❏	❏
Harlequin Romance	❏	❏	❏
Harlequin Historicals	❏	❏	❏
Harlequin Superromance	❏	❏	❏
Harlequin Intrigue	❏	❏	❏
Harlequin Presents	❏	❏	❏
Harlequin Temptation	❏	❏	❏
Harlequin Blaze	❏	❏	❏
Silhouette Special Edition	❏	❏	❏
Silhouette Romance	❏	❏	❏
Silhouette Intimate Moments	❏	❏	❏
Silhouette Desire	❏	❏	❏

2. Which of the following best describes why you bought *this book?* One answer only,
please.

the picture on the cover	❏	the title	❏
the author	❏	the line is one I read often	❏
part of a miniseries	❏	saw an ad in another book	❏
saw an ad in a magazine/newsletter	❏	a friend told me about it	❏
I borrowed/was given this book	❏	other: _____	❏

3. Where did you buy *this book?* One answer only, please.

at Barnes & Noble	❏	at a grocery store	❏
at Waldenbooks	❏	at a drugstore	❏
at Borders	❏	on eHarlequin.com Web site	❏
at another bookstore	❏	from another Web site	❏
at Wal-Mart	❏	Harlequin/Silhouette Reader	❏
at Target	❏	Service/through the mail	
at Kmart	❏	used books from anywhere	❏
at another department store or mass merchandiser	❏	I borrowed/was given this book	❏

4. On average, how many Harlequin and Silhouette books do you buy at one time?

I buy _____ books at one time	❏
I rarely buy a book	❏

MRQ403SIM-1A

5. How many times per month do you shop for any *Harlequin and/or Silhouette* books?
One answer only, please.

1 or more times a week	❏	a few times per year	❏
1 to 3 times per month	❏	less often than once a year	❏
1 to 2 times every 3 months	❏	never	❏

6. When you think of your ideal heroine, which *one* statement describes her the best?
One answer only, please.

She's a woman who is strong-willed	❏	She's a desirable woman	❏
She's a woman who is needed by others	❏	She's a powerful woman	❏
She's a woman who is taken care of	❏	She's a passionate woman	❏
She's an adventurous woman	❏	She's a sensitive woman	❏

7. The following statements describe types or genres of books that you may be
interested in reading. Pick *up to 2 types* of books that you are most interested in.

I like to read about truly romantic relationships	❏
I like to read stories that are sexy romances	❏
I like to read romantic comedies	❏
I like to read a romantic mystery/suspense	❏
I like to read about romantic adventures	❏
I like to read romance stories that involve family	❏
I like to read about a romance in times or places that I have never seen	❏
Other: _____	❏

*The following questions help us to group your answers with those readers who are
similar to you. Your answers will remain confidential.*

8. Please record your year of birth below.

19 ____

9. What is your marital status?

single ❏   married ❏   common-law ❏   widowed ❏
divorced/separated ❏

10. Do you have children 18 years of age or younger currently living at home?

yes ❏   no ❏

11. Which of the following best describes your employment status?

employed full-time or part-time ❏   homemaker ❏   student ❏
retired ❏   unemployed ❏

12. Do you have access to the Internet from either home or work?

yes ❏   no ❏

13. Have you ever visited eHarlequin.com?

yes ❏   no ❏

14. What state do you live in?

_____

15. Are you a member of Harlequin/Silhouette Reader Service?

yes ❏   Account # _____   no ❏   MRQ403SIM-1B

She could never escape
the evil of her past…

New York Times
bestselling author

SHARON SALA

Street artist Jade has spent her entire life running from the terrifying childhood she endured in a cult. When she is found and reunited with her father by ex-cop Luke Kelly, it seems that all her troubles are behind her—Jade finally feels safe in the security of her family home, with the love of a good man.

What no one realizes is that there is a man lurking in the darkness who would rather kill than let Jade reveal the secrets of her past. And now that she's stopped running, he knows exactly where to find her.

Out of the Dark

"Spellbinding narrative…Sala lives up to her reputation
with this well-crafted thriller."
—*Publishers Weekly* on *Remember Me*

Available the first week of October 2003, wherever paperbacks are sold!

#1255 A QUESTION OF INTENT—Merline Lovelace
To Protect and Defend

Tough cop Jill Bradshaw trusted no one—especially
Dr. Cody Richardson, whom she thought was out to sabotage
the secret military project she was guarding. Then she came
down with a mysterious virus, and Cody was the only one who
could help her. Could she put her suspicions aside and let him in?

#1256 CRIME AND PASSION—Marie Ferrarella
Cavanaugh Justice

Detective Clay Cavanaugh had never been too serious about
women—except for Ilene O'Hara, who had abruptly broken off their
relationship six years ago. Now Ilene was in danger and Clay had
been assigned to keep her safe. But just as he began to fall in love
with her again, he discovered a shocking secret from their past....

#1257 STRATEGIC ENGAGEMENT—Catherine Mann
Wingmen Warriors

Air force pilot Daniel Baker would do anything to smuggle his
orphaned half brothers out of a Middle Eastern country. But when he
cracked open a wooden crate and found an extra stowaway—
his tempting ex-fiancée, Mary Elise McRae—he realized he was
getting much more than he'd bargained for....

#1258 AIM FOR THE HEART—Ingrid Weaver
Eagle Squadron

As an intelligence specialist for Delta Force, Captain Sarah Fox
was sent to Stockholm to guard Dr. Hawkins Lemay. An assassin
wanted to stop the brilliant scientist's cutting-edge research, and it
was Sarah's job to stop the assassin. But how was she supposed to
deal with the knowledge that Hawkins could stop her heart?

#1259 MIDNIGHT RUN—Linda Castillo

When police detective Jack LaCroix was unjustly convicted of
his partner's murder, he knew the only person who could help
him was assistant prosecuting attorney Landis McAllister. Trouble
was, the woman he'd once loved passionately believed he'd killed
her brother in cold blood. Could they confront their churning
emotions—and unmask the true culprit—before time ran out?

#1260 THE TIE THAT BINDS—Laura Gale

Rachel Neuman spent five years trying to forget about her failed
marriage to college sweetheart Lucas. But now the daughter that
Rachel had kept secret was in danger, and Lucas was the only
person Rachel could turn to for help. Could they overcome their
troubled past in time to save their child—and revive their marriage?

SIMCNM1003